Laughing Wolf

To Gershom, Yehuda, and Miriam
Yeladim ze simcha

Laughing Wolf
Nicholas Maes

DUNDURN PRESS
TORONTO

Editor: Michael Carroll
Copy Editor: Shannon Whibbs
Design: Jennifer Scott
Printer: Webcom

Library and Archives Canada Cataloguing in Publication

Maes, Nicholas, 1960-
    Laughing wolf / by Nicholas Maes.

ISBN 978-1-55488-385-1

    I. Title.

PS8626.A37 L38 2009   jC813'.6   C2009-900505-0

1   2   3   4   5   13   12   11   10   09

Conseil des Arts du Canada   **Canada Council for the Arts**   Canadä   **ONTARIO ARTS COUNCIL CONSEIL DES ARTS DE L'ONTARIO**

We acknowledge the support of the **Canada Council for the Arts** and the **Ontario Arts Council** for our publishing program. We also acknowledge the financial support of the **Government of Canada** through the **Book Publishing Industry Development Program** and **The Association for the Export of Canadian Books**, and the **Government of Ontario** through the **Ontario Book Publishers Tax Credit program**, and the **Ontario Media Development Corporation**.

Care has been taken to trace the ownership of copyright material used in this book. The author and the publisher welcome any information enabling them to rectify any references or credits in subsequent editions.

J. Kirk Howard, President

Printed and bound in Canada.
www.dundurn.com

Dundurn Press
3 Church Street, Suite 500
Toronto, Ontario, Canada
M5E 1M2

Gazelle Book Services Limited
White Cross Mills
High Town, Lancaster, England
LA1 4XS

Dundurn Press
2250 Military Road
Tonawanda, NY
U.S.A. 14150

Chapter One

*M*arcus Licinius Crassus was standing in the street, surrounded by two hundred slaves who were holding buckets and awaiting his signal. Before him was an insula, a badly built apartment block of brick and timber, overcrowded, unhygienic, and easy to catch fire. That explained why its middle stories were ablaze and threatening to spread the flames everywhere.

Next to Crassus was the building's owner. As tenants on the upper floors pleaded to be rescued, and a crowd gathered to watch the drama, and pedestrians cursed because the street was blocked, he turned to Crassus and tugged at the great man's toga. "I'll sell it for a million denarii and not a sestertius less."

"Ten thousand denarii."

"Ten? Are you mad? Five minutes ago you offered me fifty thousand ..."

"And five minutes from now I'll offer you a mere three thousand."

"This is robbery, Marcus Licinius! I'll not have anyone forcing my hand ...!"

"Then I'll leave with my slaves and you can watch your building burn."

"This is preposterous...!"

"Eight thousand denarii.*"*

"Eight! But you just offered me ten! What effrontery! No, wait! Eight it is! Douse the fire and she's yours for eight ....!"

At the blast of a whistle Felix started from his reverie. He steadied the book that was slipping off his lap — a leather-bound edition of Plutarch's *Life of Crassus* — and sat up in his g-pod. Why had the whistle sounded? And was it his imagination or were they hovering in mid-air? He glanced at an info board and saw that, sure enough, their velocity stood at zero MPH.

He glanced at his reflection in a Teledata screen. A serious-looking face stared back, its eyes blue-green and brimming with confusion, the nose long and bony (exactly like his father's), the hair straw-coloured, and the chin sharp and dimpled. With a grunt of impatience he engaged the screen and murmured, "External monitor."

Almost instantly he was looking at a view outside the shuttle. Below him was the coast of Greenland — it was covered in piping and switching stations but was otherwise uninhabitable. On impulse he said, "Pan three hundred and sixty degrees," and the scene changed abruptly, revealing pale blue sky, cumulus clouds and … Wait. Over there, at NNW 315 degrees, a Medevac was flying toward them, its blue flashers signaling a Code A health priority. What …?

"Honoured passengers," a voice announced, "Inter-City Services regrets to inform you that Shuttle 947, from Rome to Toronto, is experiencing a medical crisis on board. A Medevac will be docking in fifty seconds and will convey the affected passenger to the nearest Health Facility. Service is expected to resume momentarily. All g-force pods have been hermetically sealed and will disengage on the completion of our disinfectant protocols. We apologize for the inconvenience and appreciate your patience."

Felix was bewildered. How could a Health Priority develop in mid-flight? Citizens were scanned for health anomalies at home, at every Portal and before any shuttle took flight, to prevent emergencies like this from occurring. Why hadn't this illness been caught in advance? And what did "disinfectant protocols" mean?

He felt a vibration. On the screen the Medevac was beside the shuttle and extending an Evac-tube to its roof. A moment later, halfway down the aisle, a circular panel of the roof swivelled open and a Flexbot arm appeared inside the shuttle. Seizing a pod six rows down from Felix, it maneuvered it to the ceiling egress and into the tube that joined the crafts together. Felix spied the patient — an elderly man. His head was slumped and he was encrusted with blisters; they were red and covered every inch of his skin.

Wishing he could help this man, Felix watched as the panel on the ceiling closed. Seconds later his g-pod trembled as the Medevac drew away from the craft.

"This system is so old," a voice spoke over his pod's speaker. Glancing around, he spotted a teen his age who was seated across the aisle from him. He was tall, big-boned, and confident-looking. His features, too, were unnervingly calm, a result of the ERR (Emotion Range Reduction) he'd undergone. And his dark eyes were sparkling from his retinal upgrades.

"My name is Stephen Gowan," he said, "Does it mean something to you?"

"No."

"Then you obviously aren't a programmer. I placed first in the North American Advanced Algorithmic series and work now as a consultant in Rome. In any event, the software on this shuttle is M4. You know what that means?"

"No."

"It was installed in 2210 and hasn't been upgraded. Three whole years without a partial upgrade! That explains why the sensors didn't catch that man's illness — although it's odd his home monitor didn't detect it either."

Felix was going to ask if he'd seen the man's blisters, but with a resonant hum the shuttle accelerated westward. Greenland was fading on the Teledata screen and the Medevac itself was just a blip in the distance. But … how strange. A blue haze was streaming from its rear exhaust, a sign that it had switched to its fusion thrusters. That happened when a craft was leaving the earth's atmosphere and why would the Medevac travel off-planet instead of delivering the patient to Stockholm or Oslo? Before Felix could work this puzzle out, Stephen Gowan spoke again.

"What's that?" he asked, pointing to Felix's lap.

"This?" Felix asked, holding up the *Life of Crassus*, "It's a book."

"A real book? Like the ones you see in museums?"

"Yes."

"Hold it up so I can look at it more closely."

"It was printed four hundred years ago," Felix explained, pressing the book against the pod's membrane.

"What's that funny writing?" Stephen asked, wrinkling his nose in curiosity.

"On the right you have classical Greek; on the left is a version in Latin."

"What are Greek and Latin?"

"They're languages that were spoken in ancient times."

"You mean, before everyone learned Common Speak?"

"Before that, even. Plutarch wrote this work two thousand years ago."

With a look of disbelief Stephen asked how he had come across the book. Felix explained that his father ran the world's last Book Repository and had filled their home with stacks of tomes. His father was also trained in Greek and Latin — there were only two such experts alive in the world — and had been teaching them to Felix for the last eleven years, from the day he'd turned four and been old enough to read. He'd also been studying these civilizations, hence his frequent trips to Rome.

"Why not use a Portadoc? It's easier to carry and holds every text that's been written, including Blutarch's books."

"Plutarch. My father won't allow me. He says a book enhances the pleasure of reading because the contents seem unique and important, whereas a Portadoc jumbles everything together."

"Your dad sounds old-fashioned."

"That's for sure. If he could, he'd stop all weather regulation, protein synthesis, retinal upgrades, synapse modification, ERR, genetic transference ..."

"Has he ever had a real job?" Stephen smirked.

"Ten years ago he uncovered a temple in France. It was hidden from sight for two thousand years until he discovered its existence through an old Roman text."

"What's a temple?"

"It's a building where people gathered and gave thanks to ... they communicated with something they called gods."

"The way we admire Reason on World Union day?"

"Yes. Something like that."

"That sounds exciting," he said, implying the exact opposite with his tone, "but I think we've arrived." As if to confirm his observation, a voice announced the shuttle had docked in Toronto's Central Depot and passengers should disembark at their leisure. There was no further mention of "disinfectant protocols."

"Nice to meet you," Felix called to Stephen who, now that the seals on his pod had opened, was standing in the aisle and hurrying away, as if anxious to escape this talk of books and ancient temples. When he failed to answer, Felix shrugged and packed away his book.

It was the same old story. As soon as people learned about his interest in the past, they assumed he was crazy and refused to talk to him further. His father suffered from the exact same problem — apart from his wife, he didn't have any friends — and was always warning Felix that their studies of the past would lead to ridicule and isolation.

By now the shuttle was empty. With a sigh, Felix climbed to his feet, headed to an exit, and made his way into the station. As always, it was crowded with people from all over the globe, Buenos Aires, Nairobi, Jerusalem, Mecca. Moving toward a Dispersion Portal, he admired the totalium vault overhead, then let his glance drift to the lower western wall, part of which was built on the building's earliest foundations that could be dated to a time when people travelled by train. His father, too, had once mentioned a door that led to something called the subway system, a network of tunnels served by underground transport. Felix had always wanted to explore this system, but the law clearly stated that this subterranean area was strictly off limits.

He joined a lineup at the Dispersion Portal. As passengers were catabolized in the doorframe's wave of current, he thought about the *Life of Crassus* and how he had to finish it before his father arrived home …

Wait. What was that? A short distance off, a woman had stumbled — one moment she'd been walking; the next she had collapsed to the floor. Had she slipped …? No, she was lying in a motionless heap. As the crowd paused and wondered what to make of this scene — their ERR prevented them from reacting promptly — Felix started forward to offer his assistance. He'd taken just a couple of steps when two Service Units pulled up and stopped him in his tracks. Signaling that this was another Health Priority, they ordered people to keep away from the woman. What …?

The crowd was backing off. The two units had formed a stretcher between them and lifted the woman onto its surface. As they floated soundlessly toward an exit, Felix glimpsed the woman's hands: the fingertips were crimson.

The room returned to normal. With the Service Units gone, the travellers hastened to their docking ports. For his part, Felix retreated to the Portal and, moments later, was poised at the head of the line.

"Destination, please?" a voice asked politely, as the Portal's turquoise current swirled, like water on the verge of freezing over.

"Area 2, Sector 4, Building 9," Felix answered.

"Processing," the voice announced. Then a moment later, "Please advance."

Felix stepped into the field. In the instant it took his atoms to be scrambled, dispatched across the city and reconfigured in the Portal outside his home, he just had time to register the thought that something was askew in their carefully ordered world.

Chapter Two

*C*rassus was standing in front of his tent. He was dressed
in a sculpted breastplate of silver, a helmet with a horse's
crest and a blood-red cloak whose folds reached his calves.
His face was stern as he eyed his legate Mummius. Ten
metres away, five hundred soldiers were waiting at attention; despite their ramrod posture, they were ill at ease.

"Spartacus worsted you and your legions?"

"Yes, sir. He attacked us from two sides at once."

"And you lost three thousand men?"

"That's correct, imperator."

"And these cowards dropped their arms as they fled
from the slaves?"

"Yes, sir. But with all due respect, Spartacus has beaten
two other armies —"

"Silence! Our discipline is slipping and must be restored!"

Eyeing his troops, Crassus told them to muster into fifty groups of ten. With typical Roman efficiency, they organized themselves within a matter of seconds. Strolling past these ranks, Crassus selected a single man from every decade, until fifty troops stood apart from the others.

"Sir!" Mummius pleaded. "Not a decimation! It wasn't our fault …!"

"Quiet!" Crassus thundered. "Romans die before they flee! And if ordered to retreat, they never drop their arms! To instill these truths, these men must die. Maybe then the others will remember their training. Swords drawn!"

Instantly, the troops who hadn't been chosen unsheathed their swords. Their fifty friends stood motionless, intent on meeting death like Romans.

At a nod from Crassus the killing began….

"Excuse me, Felix. Might I make a suggestion?"

At the sound of Mentor's voice, Felix looked up from the *Life of Crassus*. As soon as he'd arrived home, he'd greeted Mentor, "purified" himself in an ultraviolet scan and settled at a table to finish studying for his lesson. He still had thirteen chapters to go.

"Of course you can, Mentor."

"According to my sensors, you are low on protein."

"I am a little hungry. I wouldn't mind a fruit shake, please."

"My thoughts exactly. Processing time, forty-five seconds."

Felix smiled as Mentor's circuitry hummed. The sound brought back a host of happy memories. Mentor was a 3L Domestic System and had been installed in the house when Felix had been born. His father hadn't wanted a machine to tend his son, but had soon agreed that Mentor was a marvel, feeding Felix, guarding him, and teaching him to speak. Over the years new versions had appeared on the market, ones with many more features than Mentor, but Felix had refused to replace his friend. "Mentor's part of the family," he'd insisted, and his parents had agreed to hang onto this system.

"Here is your shake," Mentor spoke, producing the drink from a nearby dispenser. Seating himself in the kitchen, Felix sipped his drink.

"Thank you, Mentor. It's delicious as always."

"Did you have an interesting day?"

"I studied several temples in the Roman Forum."

"After you have read with your father, we must go over some physics."

"Fine, Mentor, fine. By the way, a man fell ill on the shuttle home and was picked up by a Medevac. And a woman collapsed in the Toronto depot."

"That is unusual. I hope these events did not prove too upsetting."

"No, well, I don't know. I hope those people are okay."

That said, Felix finished his shake and placed the glass in Mentor's hygiene recess. As he climbed to his feet, Mentor sterilized the cup and cleaned the counter with an ultraviolet "burst."

"Have you viewed your mother's message?" the computer asked.

"Not yet. I was intending to watch it when my father comes home."

"My records reveal your father viewed it at work."

"Oh. In that case, I'll look at it now."

Felix entered the living room and approached a flashing Holo-port. Moments later, light cascaded from sixteen lasers and assumed the shape of his mother's lean features. Her face displayed its usual animation and Felix grinned as the hologram began to speak. As always happened when he viewed such recordings, he shivered at the thought that she was standing on Jupiter's moon, Ganymede.

"Hello, my sweets," the hologram spoke. "I would have called sooner but the interference is terrible. We've also had some problems with the units — the oxygen leads are inefficient — but have managed at last to bring them on line. We now have fifty portables up and the colony's impressive, if I say so myself."

Felix's heart surged. He was proud of his mother. As the chief engineer for CosmoComm, a company that specialized in off-world projects, she was always travelling to distant regions, Mars, Deimos, the moon, and Ganymede, to ensure new portables were properly installed. Before her departure they'd toured the Clavius observatory, home to the earth's biggest space telescope. Studying a screen that had projected scenes of Ganymede's surface, they'd detected a tiny cluster of lights, from the outpost erected by the region's first explorers. Barely able to control her excitement, she had revealed that she loved to construct portables because they formed the foundations for future cities and would spread human life even farther afield.

"Apart from the units, there's not much else to report," she went on. "No, wait. Two days ago we were struck by a comet. It shook the moon's surface and blasted a crater over two miles wide. But other than that, my routines are the same. I miss you badly and can't wait to return. I'm getting tired of the same old view. Here, let me adjust the camera so you can see for yourself."

His mother's face vanished and an alien landscape took shape. In the foreground was a plain of ice, with a brown hue due to the atmosphere's ions. In the distance were hulking crags of rock, the result of prehistoric crater collisions: their rough-hewn peaks craned up to the sky, desperate to catch a glimpse of the sun, which wobbled into view once a week for three hours. Of course there wasn't any greenery present — no trees, no shrubs, not a single blade of grass. And because there was a total absence of wind, everything was preternaturally still, as if Felix were looking at a photograph or painting.

Jupiter was hovering above this landscape, seemingly within arm's reach of its moon. It was … vast. At one stage the camera was pointed straight at the planet and its bulk took up nine-tenths of the sky. Like its moon, it was beautiful but forbidding.

"Lonely, isn't it?" she said, appearing again, "And do you know what the earth looks like from here? It's no different from one of a billion stars. I sometimes find it hard to believe that on a tiny speck of light like that there are oceans, lakes, flowers, birds, trees, buildings, and crowds of people."

Felix nodded and was reminded, of all things, of his father's place of work. The building contained millions of books on shelves that reached right up to the ceiling's rafters. Exploring its aisles, he imagined each volume, with its collection of ideas, represented a world in miniature and that the repository itself was a universe …

"On a more cheerful note," she added, "My job here will be finished in a month. The trip home will take at least two weeks — I'll be transferring twice, on Mars and Deimos — but in six weeks time we'll be together.

I can't wait —"

Her face dissolved and reassembled, like a pond whose surface has been broken by a pebble.

"Oh dear," she said. "The interference is increasing. I'd better say goodbye before the signal disappears. By the way, the disruption will be bad for awhile, so I might not call for the next three weeks. Take care, both of you. I love you with all —"

The hologram ended before she finished her sentence.

Felix glanced outside the living-room window. It afforded him a view of the city's downtown region, with its mile-high skyscrapers whose totalium finish reflected the afternoon light. Strange to say, he was reminded of the ruins in the Roman Forum. Decrepit piles of brick and marble, the temples, basilicas, and pockmarked arches had at one time convinced each ancient Roman that his empire and wealth would endure forever. And now? The city's aqueducts, roads, religion, buildings, and poems were long forgotten.

"You are frowning. If the sun is bothering you, I can tint the window."

"That's okay, Mentor. I'm enjoying the view."

"It is very fine."

"Populations think their ways will last forever. But I bet these buildings will vanish one day, like the Parthenon, the pyramids, or the Coliseum."

"A totalium structure should last eight hundred and sixty-two years on average."

"That's not what I mean. I'm saying we don't care about the people before us. A hundred years from now, who'll remember we existed?"

"Forgive me, Felix. I have not been programmed to address such feelings."

"Never mind. It's my mother's message. They always turn me inside out."

"You should sit outside until your father arrives. The tranquility will you do good."

"That's a fine idea, Mentor. I'll follow your suggestion."

Retrieving the *Life of Crassus*, Felix approached a door, which Mentor swiftly opened. Outside was a spiral staircase that led into a well-trimmed garden. As he stared into the greenery below, Felix was thinking that he'd lied to Mentor. His mother's call didn't bother him so much as the collapse of those two people that day. His instincts told him something odd was going on.

Still, he had his lesson to think of. Descending the stairs, he put his worries aside and pretended he was entering the distant past.

Crassus was standing in the thick of his army, forty thousand men, all told. They were in Assyria, in an empty plain, with the nearest source of water some ten miles distant. A small Parthian army crowned the hills before him. An hour ago their ranks had been thicker and their archers had fired constant volleys of arrows, pinning every Roman down and preventing battle at close quarters. Finally his son had led a cavalry charge and, in true Roman fashion, beaten the enemy back. Proud of his son's manliness, Crassus was awaiting his return.

"We should leave," his legate Cassius advised. "Before the enemy regroups."

"I told you already," Crassus growled, "when Publius returns, we'll proceed to Carrhae."

"Where is he? He should have been back. If we don't leave soon …"

"We stay until he's here!" Crassus thundered. "If not for his charge, we'd be riddled with arrows and …"

A reverberation of drums interrupted — the Parthian way of sounding an attack. On the hill before them a blinding flash shone forth and a cloud of dust filled most of the sky: waves of Parthians marched into sight, archers in front, cataphracts behind, their heavy armour impervious to spear and gladius.

"We should have left," Cassius muttered.

"Where's my son?" Crassus clamoured. "And where are my horsemen?"

As if in answer, the cataphracts raised their pikes on

*high. On each was fixed the head of a Roman. And there,
on the tallest pike … Crassus would have groaned had his
thirst allowed: staring back at him, his eyes fearfully wide
in death, was the severed head of his beloved boy.*

    *As Crassus hid his face, the Parthians closed in for the
kill …*

"Felix!"

    Seated beneath an apple tree, Felix raised his eyes
from the *Life of Crassus* and watched his father slowly
draw near. Dressed in a black Zacron suit — his taste in
clothes was very old-fashioned — Mr. Taylor projected
an air of formality yet was clearly pleased to be in the
garden. The abundance of green was such a treat for his
eyes, the grass, the shrubs, the two fruit trees, both of
which were starting to blossom. A wall of bushes was
broken here and there to accommodate flowers or the
bust of a thinker. And along the garden's boundaries was
a high brick wall that blocked out everything except the
sky's expanse and the meandering clouds.

    With its vegetation and simple fixtures, it was hard
to believe this sanctuary was perched on a terrace fifteen
stories above street level.

    "*Vale fili mi.*"

    "*Vale pater.*"

These greetings exchanged, Felix eyed his father and
was surprised to see how tired he looked. Instead of
standing with his impeccably straight posture, his shoulders were stooped and his neck drooped slightly, as if his
head were too much of a burden to carry. And his eyes
were ringed and lacked their usual lustre.

"Are you okay?" Felix asked with a note of concern,
"You look tired."

"I am tired, but there's work to do."

"You saw mom's hologram? She'll be home in six
weeks."

"Yes I saw it. It's wonderful news."

"What's that?" Felix asked, pointing to a book his dad
was carrying. It was small and bound in bright blue leather.

"It's nothing really," his father said vaguely. "A work
of history, that's all."

"By whom?"

"Sextus Pullius Aceticus."

"Aceticus? The vinegary one? I've never heard of him."

"He's not well known," his father agreed. "And this
edition in my pocket is particularly rare. Still, he's …
interesting."

"What period does he cover?"

"We'll discuss it later," Mr. Taylor said dismissively.
"Let's start and read about Spartacus's struggle. His
story is why I assigned the *Life of Crassus*. Over the last

few days this era has come to obsess me."

"Okay," Felix agreed. While his dad took a seat, he selected the right chapter and translated from the Latin into Common Speak.

He read how Spartacus had been a gladiator in the town of Capua. His owner Batiatus had treated his slaves badly, confining them and beating them often. Spartacus and others were determined to escape. Using a mix of kitchen utensils, they stormed their guards, fled the school, and armed themselves with swords and spears before venturing due south. When the praetor Clodius led three thousand troops against them, Spartacus and his companions crushed this army, gained a cache of weapons for themselves, and attracted many more slaves to their cause.

"The Romans don't come off well," Felix said.

"They most certainly don't," his father agreed.

"They had slaves and encouraged gladiatorial games ...."

"They have their better aspects, too. It's strange how civilization can contain such savage elements."

Felix continued. A second Roman army arrived — it consisted of six thousand soldiers — and Spartacus promptly routed it, too. By this time twenty thousand slaves had joined him. Aware he couldn't beat the Romans forever, he led his troops as far as the Alps and advised them to leave Italy and return to their homelands. They refused, preferring to plunder instead. As they roamed the countryside and attracted more slaves, they killed Rome's soldiers by the tens of thousands.

"There's so much death," Felix lamented.

"It isn't pretty," his father sighed, "But it's important to know the truth about ourselves. If we want to grasp humanity in all its dimensions, we have to see ourselves as we are, and not as we would like ourselves to be."

"I suppose," Felix said, with a lack of conviction. "I'm just glad I haven't experienced this bloodshed for myself."

He read how a fourth Roman army was mustered, a huge one under the command of Crassus. The slaves marched to the toe of Italy where they planned to hire boats and sail to Sicily. Unfortunately, these ships failed to appear and Crassus boxed them in with a wall that was eight feet tall and twelve miles long. Heavy fighting followed. While the slaves smashed the wall and forced their way north, thirty thousand souls were lost in the process. In a final battle by the Silarus River, Spartacus took a gamble and charged the Roman army: the odds were stacked against him, however, and the Romans cut his troops to pieces. The gladiator himself died in combat. The surviving slaves, six thousand men, were crucified by Crassus along the Appian Way, as a warning to all slaves that their attempts to revolt would be ruthlessly dealt with. And so ended the famous slave rebellion.

Felix paused. He was going to ask his father what he thought of Spartacus but, as he looked up from his book, his mouth dropped open. His father was ... sleeping! What on earth ...? Through all their many lessons together, not once had his father nodded off on the job. In fact, when Felix himself had been tempted to nap, how many times had he been told that their lessons were too precious to waste a single moment snoozing?

Felix blushed. His father was snoring. Closing his book, he climbed to his feet and tiptoed toward the start of the garden. His initial impulse had been to wake his father, but his face was pale and he looked exhausted and it seemed a good idea to let him sleep until supper.

He retreated to the staircase. As he climbed its steps, he thought about the people who had collapsed that day and how their prostrate forms resembled his father's. Not that he was worried: if his father were sick, Mentor would have caught it.

A loud, raucous cawing broke in on his thoughts. Spinning about, he looked around him. What was that racket ...? Oh!

A crow had alighted on the tree's top branch. Its plumage was black as pitch and its beak looked sharp and menacing. Felix was amazed. Crows were rarely seen in the city — they had left when humans had started controlling the weather.

But there was something else. For a moment, he thought the air about his father had split in half, revealing a figure who looked ... exactly like himself. He shook himself vigorously: no, the apparition was gone.

But the crow was still there. As if aware of Felix's stare, it perched itself beside his father. "*Aagh, aagh, aagh,*" it cried, as if addressing him directly. A shiver ran down Felix's spine. The crow was poised to his father's right: according to Roman traditions, a sighting like this was a terrible sign.

"Go away!" Felix yelled.

"*Aagh, aagh, aagh!*" the crow continued.

"Go away!" he repeated, "Leave my father alone!"

"*Aagh, aagh, aagh!*" the crow called, more insistently than ever. Abandoning the bough, he alighted on his dad's right shoulder. And still his father continued to sleep.

This was more than Felix could bear. Hurrying down the staircase, he rushed toward the tree. Observing his approach, the crow finally took wing. It circled the tree and cawed once or twice, as if deliberately insulting Felix further ... unless it was warning him of trouble ahead. Tracing one last circle, the bird shot into the sky and, seconds later, was a point in the distance.

Although he didn't believe in ghosts or superstitions, Felix had to concentrate to keep his legs from shaking.

Chapter Three

When Felix awoke the next morning, his nervousness was gone. He'd slept like a log, it was beautiful outside, and the headlines on the news communicator spoke of sports, off-world projects, and upgrades to the weather template. There was no mention of people collapsing at random and that meant yesterday's crisis had passed. He would have joked with Mentor had they not been studying physics together.

"Explain the importance of Johann Clavius."

"He discovered the unified field equation in 2165."

"Good. What else?"

"By using principles of hyper-spatial geometry, he proved three particles exist that can travel faster than the speed of light."

"And what does this imply, theoretically, at least?"

"If these particles have the same magnetic spin, and are aligned along a certain vector path, their time coefficient can be transposed."

"And?"

"Theoretically, they would vanish into the past."

"And the equation for this process is …?"

"I … I … can't remember."

"Review it as you travel to Rome. And speaking of Rome, you have five minutes and fifteen seconds to catch the 8:36 shuttle."

Felix rose from the table and walked by a scanner, being sure to expose his teeth to its rays. Grabbing a copy of Virgil's *Aeneid* — whose contents he was trying to learn by heart — he approached the door to his father's bedroom.

"I'm off!" he announced.

"Are you visiting the Forum?" his father asked.

"I think I'll tour the *Domus Aurea*. But my shuttle's leaving. I'll see you later this afternoon. Dad? Did you hear me?"

"Yes," his father spoke. "Have a great day, *fili mi*."

"You, too. Bye."

A minute later, Felix was exiting his building. He chuckled. His shuttle was leaving in ninety-three seconds yet he would catch it because there was hardly any lineup at the Portal. Was this his lucky day?

At Central Depot he was in such a rush that there wasn't time to take in his surroundings. It was only when he'd clambered on board that he noticed the craft was strangely empty. Normally the aisles were packed with commuters, to the point where the auto-steward would have to guide him to a seat, whereas today less than half the g-pods were full. Was there a public holiday or something?

Unless ....

Before his thoughts could sour, Stephen Gowan waved him over. He was sitting at the front of the craft and the pod across from him happened to be vacant. Did he want to apologize for his brusqueness yesterday?

"Hello!" Felix greeted him, seating himself.

"It feels ... busy," Stephen said, with a look of confusion.

"Busy?" Felix laughed, mistaking his intention, "How can you say that when the shuttle's half empty?"

"Is it cold in here?" Stephen asked. His hands were shaking slightly.

"It feels normal to me."

He was going to ask Stephen where he worked in Rome, but his g-pod's membrane closed and the floor vibrated — signs the shuttle had left its moorings. Activating an external monitor, he watched as a tractor beam steered them from the depot and lifted them above the downtown district. He glanced into the offices that drifted past.

"Felix," Stephen gasped over his pod's speaker, "Have you undergone ERR?"

"No. When the time came to decide, I opted out at my father's suggestion."

"So … you know fear?"

"Well, I experience it from time to time. You must remember it, too, from when you were young." He was gazing at the monitor still. The shuttle had floated past a line of windows yet he'd glimpsed a total of fifteen people. Where was everybody? And instead of accelerating, the shuttle was braking.

"Beneath my ERR, I'm afraid," Stephen whispered.

"Afraid of what?"

"There's something inside me. It's about to explode."

"What's inside you? You look kind of pale."

"It's too late. It's taking over …."

Slumping forward, he exposed the whites of his eyes. The shuttle halted and a whistle sounded.

"Honoured passengers," the auto-steward spoke, "InterCity Services regrets to inform you that Shuttle 947, from Toronto to Rome, is experiencing five medical crises on board. A Medevac will dock with us in seven seconds and convey affected passengers to a nearby Health Facility. Shuttle 947 will then return to the main depot. All g-force pods have been hermetically sealed and will disengage on the completion of our disinfectant protocols. We apologize ..."

Before the steward could finish its announcement, each Teledata screen displayed a message in bold letters: "Stay tuned for a broadcast from our Global President." A countdown appeared. One minute and ten seconds, nine, eight, seven ...

The shuttle trembled slightly. A ceiling panel above Stephen opened and a Flexbot arm shot into the cabin. Before Felix had a chance to address him, his pod was hoisted into an Evac-tube. Felix glimpsed his face and almost flinched in horror: normal just moments before, it was covered now with blood-red blisters. And his fingertips looked like they'd been steeped in red ink.

... Thirty-two, thirty-one, thirty ...

And Stephen wasn't the only one affected. Two seats behind him a man had toppled over, and a well-dressed lady further down was crumpled up, with a Portadoc lying on its side by her feet. Flexbots were busy removing them as well.

... Twelve, eleven, ten ...

Felix thought his heart would explode. What was happening? Why had all these people fainted? What did their blisters and red fingertips mean? Were they dying? Was it his turn next ...?

… Three, two, one …

As soon as the countdown expired, a face filled his screen — as well as every other screen on board the shuttle. Felix recognized Sajit Gupta at once, three-time president of the World Federation. A handsome man with a friendly manner, President Gupta was subdued at that moment.

"My fellow citizens," he spoke in a sober tone, "I'm afraid I have worrying news to deliver. Five days ago a virus came to our attention, a strain our immunologists had never seen. The Federation wasn't concerned, but quarantined its victims and set to work on finding a vaccine. Now, four days later, the virus has infected millions. A mere three people have died so far, but the rest are ill and require hospitalization. As far as any vaccine is concerned, I regret to say it has eluded us still …"

Felix gasped. This was even worse than he'd imagined.

"In an effort to contain this virus, my government has published a decree that prohibits citizens from traveling at large. We insist that you remain inside your homes, monitor your health at six-hour intervals, and obey the authorities should you suffer infection. All transportation has been cancelled forthwith, and this ban includes all off-world traffic. Failure to comply with these rules will result in arrest and immediate detention."

There was a bump as the shuttle returned to its moorings. Felix's g-pod opened, but he didn't move. He lacked the strength to budge from that spot.

"My dear citizens, over the last hundred years we have conquered hunger, war, and most diseases. Science has served us well in the past, and I feel confident it will rescue us again. In the meantime, I beg you to remain optimistic. We will eliminate this plague but we must trust in our reason. As always I wish you the best blessings I can think of, peace, rationality and constructive thoughts."

The president waved and the screen went blank. Immediately, an alarm bell rang and the steward ordered passengers to leave by the closest exit. A line of people shuffled down the aisle, quietly, calmly, betraying no fear. As Felix watched them and wrestled with his panic, he envied them their ERR. It's too bad his father was opposed …

His father! Felix leaped to his feet. Was his dad still at home or had he left for work? He'd looked frail and tired the day before and Felix prayed this didn't mean … Running down the aisle, he exited the shuttle.

The scene that confronted him in the station was ghastly. A good dozen people had collapsed to the tiles and a line of Service Units was hauling them off. A girl kept repeating she wanted to stay, but the machines had their orders and were deaf to her pleas. An older man was crawling on all fours, in an effort to escape the units' cold touch. Auto-ushers were everywhere and escorting commuters to their destinations.

The lineups at the Portals were maddeningly long. People were standing a distance from each other and covering their mouths with anything at hand — handkerchiefs, socks, baseball caps. Without warning, a woman in front of Felix fainted and the crowd instantly stepped away. They were a frightening sight with their impassive eyes and strips of fabric concealing their faces. A second person dropped, then another and another. Felix was half breathless with terror when at last he reached the head of the line.

"Destination please," a voice asked politely, as if this day were just like any other.

"Area 2, Sector 4, Building 9," Felix panted, shuddering as a lady sprouted blisters before his eyes.

"Processing," the voice announced. Then, an eternity later, "Please advance."

He almost laughed, the change was so abrupt. One moment he was being hemmed in by death; the next he was standing in front of his building and a warm sun was caressing him. He almost convinced himself he'd escaped the disaster, when he spied a figure immediately before him: half the man's body was sprawled on the pathway, while half was lying on the manicured lawn. The victim was dressed in a black Zacron suit and was clutching a book that was bound in blue leather, his fingertips a telltale scarlet. The face was turned away, but Felix knew who it was.

"Dad!" he screamed, hastening forward.

"Don't approach him!" a voice called from above. "You'll get yourself infected. Besides, a Medevac will be here soon."

Ignoring this advice, Felix ran to his father. He was very still, didn't seem to be breathing and his face was disfigured with disquieting blisters. Just as Felix was assuming the worst, Mr. Taylor opened his eyes and managed a faint smile.

"*Fili mi*. Thank goodness you're here."

"Don't speak. Save your strength."

"Felix. Listen closely. We've seen this plague before. Aceticus describes it."

"Shh," Felix soothed him, thinking he was confused. "A Medevac is on the way."

Sure enough there was a buzzing overhead and, above the treetops, a Medevac swooped near. As it hovered closer, Felix glanced into its cockpit: the sight of the auto-drive was deeply unnerving.

"Felix?"

"Yes, Dad?"

"It's all in there," his father wheezed, motioning to the book by his side. "Read it carefully. It might prove useful."

"The Medevac's above us," Felix said.

"We survived the plague once, and we can survive it again if —"

"This is Medevac OS3201," an automated voice announced, cutting Mr. Taylor off. As the vehicle hovered fifty feet above the ground, a panel opened and released a one-man stretcher that descended on a trio of miniature jets. Felix didn't like the look of this contraption: with its transparent cover and retractable arms, whose ends were equipped with metal grapplers, it resembled more a beast of prey than a medical contrivance.

"Felix," his father whispered. His voice was growing weaker.

"Yes, Dad?"

"You've made me proud. I'm lucky to have had a son like you."

"Don't give up. The doctors will help ...."

"Step aside from the patient," the voice declared. The stretcher was only four feet off the ground and was casting a shadow over Mr. Taylor. Already both its arms were extended. Felix shifted slightly, to accommodate the stretcher, but continued clutching his father.

"Read Aceticus," he gasped. His eyes were fluttering shut.

"I will. And when you return —"

"*Puer mi*, this is serious ..."

"You'll get better. Mom will return and —"

"Remember me!" his father cried.

The stretcher had landed. With mechanical efficiency, its arms seized hold of Mr. Taylor and lifted his body onto the mattress. Two bands of metal secured him in place.

"Remember me!" his father repeated, squeezing his son one final time. He then fainted and his hand slipped from Felix's fingers. There was a pneumatic hiss as the cover drew closed. Before Felix could speak, the stretcher started to rise.

"Don't go!" Felix cried. "I want to stay with my father!"

"Remain still please," a voice addressed him.

Felix had to cover his eyes. A pulsing light passed over his body and seemed to ignite his internal organs, as if the beam were entering every one of his cells. For a moment Felix couldn't breathe — he felt he was drowning in a pool of sunlight. Then the blaze quickly vanished and he opened his eyes.

"Our probes show you are uninfected," the voice said. "This vehicle is reserved for patients who are ill."

"My father needs me! He'll be lonely by himself …!"

"Transport regulations cannot be broken."

"Then tell me where you're taking him!"

"Consult Health Services for that information."

"That's ridiculous! Wait! Don't go!"

But the stretcher was inside the vessel now. And once its egress had been resealed, the craft rose quickly and fired its thrusters. A moment later it had disappeared.

Felix was dumbfounded. His father was … gone. When would he see him? He wasn't going to …?

A noisy buzzing interrupted his thoughts. A second Medevac passed and paused above a nearby building. Dozens were now visible — they seemed to occupy the heavens. In the downtown area a siren was blaring.

Felix stirred himself. Retrieving his father's blue book, he shot into their building and raced past the entrance. In the lobby he ignored a man who was prostrate on the tiles and being "prepped" by a Personal Servant. He held his breath as he rode a Vacu-lift and hurried down a hallway and paused before a security scan. And when he was safe inside the dwelling, he directed Mentor to bolt the doors and windows. Still not satisfied with these precautions, he ran to his bedroom and hid under the blankets.

And still he was sure that Death was lurking in the shadows.

Chapter Four

"Felix?"

"Yes?"

"It is five minutes to three."

"So?"

"You must step inside the Health Cell."

"You can't scan me with your sensors?"

"We have discussed that already. My sensors cannot screen for the virus."

Felix scowled. It had been two weeks since his father's collapse and the president's announcement of a global crisis. In that interval, the plague had spread so widely that the sick by far outnumbered the healthy.

Everything had changed. In keeping with the president's edict, all shuttles had been grounded, all Portals

had been closed, and it was forbidden to stray outdoors
or even open a window. That morning Felix had logged
onto the WSRS (World Satellite Reconnaissance System) and inspected cities across the globe. Each had
been abandoned: in New York, London, Hong Kong,
and Nairobi the main streets had been empty, except
for the occasional cat or dog. It was as if the planet
were one gigantic ... graveyard.

"Felix, it is now two minutes to three."

"Remind me why I need to be examined."

"Failure to submit to examination ...

"Will result in immediate incarceration. So?"

"Please, Felix. I understand you are troubled, but
you must remain focused."

Felix frowned from his perch on a couch. Ten days
earlier he'd contacted the World Health Service — it
had taken him over a week to get through — to inquire
about his father's condition. After obtaining his father's
serial number, an auto-clerk had told him that Eric Taylor, citizen 967597102-364, had succumbed to his illness. "You mean he's dead?" Felix had asked, his knees
almost buckling. Advising him to supplement his ERR
with "grief downloads," the auto-clerk had disconnected.

Since then Felix had barely stirred from the couch.

"Felix, I must insist."

"Are you sure it's time?"

"My internal clock is 99.99999763% accurate. I am off by approximately one second every century. This means it is most assuredly three p.m."

"I'm sorry, Mentor. I didn't mean to doubt you."

"There is no need to apologize. But please hurry to the Health Cell. If you fail to activate its program as required, I will be forced to notify the Health Authorities."

"Fine," Felix relented. "Let's get this over and done with."

With a sigh, he left the couch. Part of him was tempted to break the rules and be late for his "appointment." So what if the authorities hauled him off? Would incarceration be so terrible, now that his father ... his father ...

He winced. It pained him to consider that their lessons together, their exchanges in the garden, their jokes in Latin that no else could grasp, were hopelessly shattered and would never return.

"It is one minute to three."

"Stop pestering me, Mentor. I'm almost there."

"I am safeguarding your welfare, Felix. Your mother would be angry if you were arrested through my negligence."

"There. I'm in the Health Cell. You can activate the scan."

As the panel on the Health Cell closed, and its ion shower started to glow, Felix wondered when he'd hear from his mother. Because the president had cancelled all off-world flights, Mrs. Taylor was on Ganymede still. The interference, too, had been bad in recent days and communicating with her was out of the question. After learning of his father's death, Felix had been able to send a short message, informing his mother of the horrible news. She had been able to answer, but her transmission had been brief: "Felix, be brave. Your father was so proud of you. I'll be home as soon as the travel ban is lifted. Try to endure. I love you very —"

Every time Felix replayed this message, he tried to catch his mother's tears — on the hologram they resembled beads of liquid glass.

"I'm pleased to inform you that your Health Cell scan is negative. You bear no trace of the virus."

"Can I come out now?"

"Yes. Your next test is scheduled for nine p.m. I will of course inform you in advance of this appointment."

"I'm sure you will."

"Do I detect a note of sarcasm, Felix?"

"No. You detect loneliness, worry, and sadness, Mentor."

Besides Mentor, Felix had no one to talk to. There were his relatives — in Ireland, Israel and Malaysia

— but they weren't answering his holograms, a sign they too had been afflicted with the plague. He had no friends because of his strange interests, but even if they had existed, the chances were they would have fallen ill. The plague was sparing no one, and it was only a matter of time before it hit him, too.

Felix started pacing. As he shuffled from his bedroom to the central hall, he passed the door to his father's study. Normally he would have closed his eyes — he hadn't dared enter this room since his dad's disappearance — but a peculiar odor brought him to a stop. It was a strange smell, sharp, but not unpleasant. Where was it coming from? After hesitating briefly, Felix crossed the threshold.

Things were as his father had left them, the books, the pens and paper (who else wrote with a pen?), the Latin dictionary, the magnifying glass, the leather-bound armchair, the old Roman coins. And … oh. A glass of wine was resting on his desk. Was this the source of that penetrating odour?

Felix drew closer. He ran his hand along the desk's smooth surface and installed himself in its throne-like chair. The room was thick with his father's presence and Felix half expected him to walk in at that moment. Being careful not to disturb anything, he leaned forward and sniffed the contents of the glass.

It *was* the source of the smell. Over time, the wine had turned to vinegar, hence the sour, pungent aroma. Felix smiled. "Vinegary," Aceticus, was the author of the book that his father had been reading ...

His smile faded. He recalled his father's statement, how the book had something to say about the plague. "It's all in there," he'd murmured, motioning to the tome. At the time Felix had been too scared to pay attention, but he wondered now what his father had meant. He exited the study with a purposeful step.

"Would you like a game of chess?"

"Not now, Mentor. I'm looking for a book."

"What book would that be?"

"Aceticus's *Historiae*. It's thin and bound in dark blue leather."

"It is on the table next to the entrance."

"Thank you, Mentor. That's very helpful."

Felix ran to the front door and, yes, the book was there. Caressing it, he remembered with a pang how he'd seen it last in his father's hands. He opened it slowly to a page with a bookmark — the paper was yellow and dusty with age.

A paragraph jumped out at him.

The book almost slipped from his fingers. Stumbling to the couch on legs as weak as jelly, he fumbled with the book and read the passage over.

He shook his head in disbelief. Turning back three pages, he read their contents, too, studying every sentence with painstaking care. At one point he consulted a Latin lexicon, to check the exact meaning of a couple of words.

An hour passed. Mentor suggested that he eat something but Felix replied he wasn't a bit hungry. An hour later Mentor spoke again, but Felix shrugged him off.

When the old clock in the dining room struck six, Felix put the book away. He'd read the Latin ten times over and still couldn't believe the story it told. No wonder the text had absorbed his father. "*Lupus ridens*," he murmured to himself.

He considered his options. The facts he'd discovered were of vital importance and had to be brought to someone's attention but ... how? It would take days to contact the Information Bureau, and even if he did get through, the auto-clerks weren't programmed to forward his call.

But the information was crucial and he had to do something.

"You seem pensive," Mentor stated, breaking in on his thoughts.

"I have a problem," Felix answered. "I've found some information that the authorities should hear."

"It will take four days and sixteen hours to reach the Information Bureau ...."

"Yes," Felix snapped. "That's why I'm debating what my next step should be."

"On the other hand," Mentor went on, ignoring Felix's burst of temper, "you can inform the authorities by communicating with a talk-show host."

"Like whom?" Felix asked, his interest piqued.

"Monitoring," Mentor said, initiating a search of the broadcast network. "At present there are 17573 talk shows worldwide."

"I need one with a wide viewing audience ...."

"*The Angstrom Show* has ten million viewers. It is running currently on channel 213. Shall I engage the Entertainment Complex?"

"My dad hated that machine," Felix gulped.

"If your information is crucial, I am sure your father would understand."

"All right," Felix relented. "Please screen *The Angstrom Show*."

No sooner had he reached this decision than a bright light appeared above the EC console and, like clay being shaped upon a potter's wheel, assumed the form of two men sitting before a globe of the world. The blonde-haired giant in a Klytex suit was Siegfried Angstrom, the talk show's host. On his right was Dr. Lee — or so a banner proclaimed — chief director of the Science Institute.

"Let's cut to the chase," Angstrom was saying. "When will we have a cure for the plague?"

"I really can't say," Dr. Lee replied.

"Not even a rough estimate? A week? Two weeks? A month? A year?"

"As I explained, we haven't determined the virus's structure. Until we do, we can't replicate —"

The EC was starting to beep — Mentor was processing a request for connection. Felix started breathing hard. The thought suddenly struck him that, if he appeared on the show, millions would be watching. The idea made him nervous.

"... But we're running out of time," Angstrom said. "Half the population has been hit with the virus. They're getting by on life support, but that won't help if the plague keeps spreading."

"I agree. The problem is that a cure continues to elude us."

The pair kept talking. Angstrom kept hinting that the scientists were lazy, while the doctor kept repeating that his centre was doing the best it could. Every two minutes, Angstrom would let a caller speak. These people, too, were angry with the doctor and kept blaming the scientists for dragging their feet.

After watching the show for nearly an hour, Felix started thinking he was wasting his time. People were

calling from all over the globe, and the chances of connection were maybe one in a million. But no sooner had
this thought registered than the EC started flashing red.
Moments later a 3D image of Felix was visible beside
Siegfried Angstrom and the doctor.

Shocked, Felix realized he was on the air.

"Felix Taylor from Toronto is on the line," Angstrom
said. "Good evening, Felix. What's on your mind?"

"Pardon me?" Felix asked, his tongue cleaving to the
roof of his mouth.

"Don't tell me you're nervous," Angstrom jeered.
"Or maybe your ERR implants have failed?"

"I've never undergone ERR," Felix gulped, trying
hard to focus his thoughts.

"You've got to be kidding!" Angstrom growled. "In
that case, call back when you've undergone treatment or
have a grip on your nerves."

"No, I'm fine," Felix spoke, swallowing his terror.

"Okay." Angstrom smiled. "Have you a question for
our guest?"

"Actually," Felix said, inhaling deeply, "I'd like to
report a discovery I've made."

"How exciting!" Angstrom grinned. "Please share it
with our viewers."

Aware that the host was poking fun at him, Felix
described his father's routines, how he'd worked in the

Depository, brought home piles of books and taught his son both Latin and Greek. The point was, Felix added, as Angstrom shifted restlessly, that he'd stumbled on an ancient text that cast some light on the plague.

"Let me get this straight," Angstrom interrupted. "You're saying a book that was written in the past has something to say about the disaster we're facing?

"That's exactly what I'm saying."

"Then I've heard enough," Angstrom smirked, leaning forward to press the disconnect button.

"You don't understand!" Felix said sternly. "I'm saying this same plague struck two thousand years ago!"

At this news Angstrom flinched, while the doctor sat up straight in his chair.

"It will become clearer if I read to you," Felix explained, opening the *Historiae* to the page with the bookmark. Angstrom and the doctor leaned forward in their seats.

"'Two days after the death of Spartacus," he read, "a plague broke out near the town of Panarium, a small but prosperous farming centre. Without warning, people in the town fell ill. Spots erupted on their faces, their necks grew swollen, and their fingertips turned red, as if they'd been immersed in blood. Its victims also lapsed into a sleep so deep that no amount of shaking would possibly rouse them.'" Felix paused for breath and addressed

Angstrom directly. "Notice the symptoms. Facial spots, red fingertips, coma …"

"Are you a doctor?" Angstrom asked.

"No."

"Then you have no right to jump to conclusions. In fact —"

"'For a month," Felix went on reading, to prevent himself from being cut off, "the plague rampaged like a conquering army. Rich and poor fell ill, Roman and non-Roman, slave and master, honest folk and criminals. Offerings were delivered to the gods, but still the plague continued, drawing strength from every victim it claimed. Hearing of this sickness, officials in Rome grew worried. If the plague reached the capital, it would kill people by the tens of thousands. Rome's foes might attack it in its weakened state, and slaves might remember Spartacus and continue his rebellion. The fate of the empire seemed to hang in the balance.'"

"Slaves, war, invasion!" Angstrom growled, his 3D image recoiling in horror. "I think you've tried our patience enough!"

"I'm getting to the important part —"

"Finish quickly," the doctor broke in. "This talk of the past is most unpleasant."

"'In the third week of the crisis,'" Felix pressed on, "'The plague struck the capital. Within days three thousand

Romans lay dying. As officials struggled to halt the disease, and citizens prepared to flee the city, a farmer from Panarium made the strangest claim. Some months before the plague had started, his entire crop had failed. His fields had produced, not wheat and barley, but an ungainly flower called *lupus ridens*, so named because its petals resembled a laughing wolf. His neighbours had assumed he had offended the gods and refused to provide his household with grain. In desperation, the farmer had fed his family this flower, whose bulb, though bitter, was highly nutritious. The results were startling. Whereas every neighbour had fallen ill, the farmer was in perfect health. Far from being a curse, the *lupus ridens* was a blessing.'"

"What barbarians!" Angstrom snorted, "To believe in gods ...!"

"'Hearing this tale,'" Felix concluded, "'the senator Gaius Julius Caesar bought the flowers from the farmer and distributed bulbs throughout Italy. Within weeks of eating the *lupus ridens*, citizens were delivered from the brink of death: they awoke from their sleep, their spots disappeared and their red fingertips regained their normal colour. And thus it was that a simple flower saved the empire in its hour of need.'"

Felix closed the book. "So you see," he concluded, "this plague does have a cure. We only have to find this *lupus ridens* and —"

"Enough!" Angstrom cried. "How dare you mention … fairy tales! If you'd undergone ERR, you'd be thinking with your head and not your emotions!"

"This is no fairy tale!" Felix said hotly. "Just because it was written —"

"At a time when people thought the sun was a god," Angstrom sneered. "And when slavery and war were everyday occurrences."

"But the story tells us something," Felix cried. "Don't you think so, Doctor?"

"I think," the doctor mused, "that we've heard enough superstition for one day."

"My feelings exactly," Angstrom agreed. "Now if you don't mind, Felix, there are other callers on the line."

Felix was about to protest, but Angstrom pressed a button and his holographic image popped like a bubble.

As he sat on the couch without moving a muscle, other guests connected and ridiculed his tale about the *lupus ridens*. A few suggested that Mr. Taylor should be jailed for having taught his son such absolute nonsense and that all ancient texts should be thrown into a furnace. Felix asked Mentor to turn the EC off.

The sun was setting. Shadows were gathering in the room. His loneliness a crushing weight on his shoulders, Felix curled into a ball and slowly drifted off.

Chapter Five

*H*e was standing in a desert. Around him was a crowd of legionnaires, who looked tired and ... apprehensive. They were staring in front of them, with such concentration that they failed to notice Felix. Curious, he moved through their ranks, and still they continued to direct their gaze forward. What WERE they looking at?

Wait! The troops were suddenly changing: their faces were spotted, their fingertips were reddening and many were collapsing! He sprinted toward the foremost ranks where a figure was surveying the plain before him. Felix knew this was Marcus Crassus and that the battle of Carrhae was about to begin, one of Rome's more troubling defeats. Even now the Parthians were approaching, with their fifteen-foot pikes. What was on the end of each? It *couldn't be! Hoisted on high, beneath the blinding desert sun, his father's head stared lifelessly at Felix....*

Felix awoke with a cry. He'd been napping on the couch and, with the night's onset, the unit was steeped in shadow. Wait, no. A flashing light intruded from outside, and an angry buzzing was making his ears ring — as if a hive of bees had broken into their dwelling.

"Mentor? What's happening?"

The flashing light grew brighter. The buzzing, too, rose in volume, until Felix could feel his insides tingle. He struggled off the couch and studied the room. His instincts told him something was wrong.

"Mentor! Answer me! What's going on?"

Wait. Mentor's light ports weren't blinking; a sign his power had been cut. But how? The system was linked to three separate generators, and a short like this was out of the question — unless it had been engineered.

Felix's hair stood on end. Somehow someone had ... *murdered* Mentor!

"Felix Taylor!" a voice hailed him from outside, "This is Medevac 125037. We are here to transport you to a health facility."

A Medevac? Here? It was going to transport him?

Felix felt his neck and scalp bristle. There could only be one explanation: he'd come down with the virus!

He hurried to a mirror beside the front entrance. Although the only light was from the flashers outside, he peered into it anxiously and tried to spy his features. Were there blisters on his cheeks? Had his fingertips turned red? It was difficult to tell, but everything seemed normal. And far from feeling tired, he was filled with nervous energy.

"Please step onto the balcony. We have dispatched a stretcher."

No sooner were these words announced than a stretcher hovered into view, its retractable arms as threatening as ever. With a quiet but insistent hum its miniature jets steered it straight onto the balcony. Watching it with bated breath, Felix thought he must have missed his next exam and the authorities were closing in. Mentor, poor Mentor, had been right all along and ...

How odd. The old-fashioned clock read 8:46 p.m. So he *hadn't* missed his appointment yet. But then why was a Medevac paying him a visit ...?

"Please step onto the balcony. You are wasting precious time."

Felix unsealed the balcony door — a task Mentor would have normally performed. As he stepped outside and savoured the fresh air, the stretcher's lid opened with a snake-like hiss. Spying it, Felix was taken aback. Once he climbed inside it and the lid wheeled closed, he'd be linked to a series of soul-less machines.

"Lie down on the stretcher," the voice enjoined him.

He didn't want to go. Earlier, he hadn't cared if the authorities swooped in, but now that his freedom was endangered he was sorely afraid. And not just afraid: he was angry and defiant.

"Lie down on the stretcher," the voice insisted. "We are falling behind schedule."

"You're mistaken," he yelled back. "I don't have the disease."

"Lie down!" the voice repeated. "We will not ask you again."

"Can't you hear me? I'm not sick. And why did you disable my domestic system?"

He sensed its approach at the very last instant. Glancing around, he saw a fist-sized sphere had stationed itself behind him. It was a BISDM — a Brain Interference Signal Delivery Mechanism. Before he could duck or jump to one side, a wall of energy seemed to engulf him.

As a wave of black struck him, he was thinking he'd never open his eyes again.

"You can open your eyes."

There was a high-pitched whine far in the background and the continuous beeping of a signal exchange. A blast of air felt nice against his cheek.

"Come on. Hurry. My father's going to test you once we've reached the stratosphere. Open your eyes and talk to me."

Without stirring, Felix struggled to puzzle things out. His brain had been shocked and his body flung onto a stretcher. And now a Medevac was conveying him to a facility in orbit, unless his refusal to co-operate would land him in jail. Either way, he didn't care. The trick was to keep his eyes firmly closed....

"Open your eyes!"

"Stop bossing me around!" he shouted, opening his eyes in spite of himself. To his surprise he was staring at a girl his age, with short, blonde hair, hazel-green eyes, and a chin that suggested she was very self-composed. He also noticed the stretcher's lid was open.

"The lid is open," he stated. "So I'm not infected."

"No."

"So why am I here? Why did you shock me? Why did you kill Mentor? And who are you anyway?"

"My name is Carolyn Manes. But never mind that. You sound angry, emotional."

"What do you expect?"

"I mean, you haven't undergone ERR."

"No. On my father's advice, I dispensed with it."

"It must be odd to experience emotion. My father says it can hamper one's judgment, but at the same time it can lead to valuable insight."

"Who's your father?"

"He's a general and is in charge of the Temporal Projection Matrix."

"This is all very interesting, but what's it all about? Why did a Medevac ...?"

"No one can know about the TPM. That's why we've faked that you're ill and hauled you off in a medical transport."

"You've lost me ..."

"My father's coming," she said. "We'll talk later."

Without another word, she hurried to the far end of the Medevac.

Seconds later, a large, well-groomed man approached. He had short, grey hair, light green eyes, a chiselled chin and, apart from his Chromine uniform, looked the spitting image of his daughter. Beside him was an older man with a lavish white beard. He was thin and wrinkled, and was dressed in a suit that Mr. Taylor might have worn. Although Felix had heard of glasses before, he'd never met anyone who actually wore them. The lenses were distorting the man's bloodshot eyes.

"I'm General Manes," the man in the uniform announced, grasping Felix's hand and yanking him out of the stretcher.

"Hello," Felix said in a strangled voice.

"This gentleman here," the general continued, "is Professor MacPherson. Like you, he joined our project only recently."

"Project?"

"I'll explain in good time. Just now I'd like you to say something in Latin."

"Excuse me?"

"You claimed on *The Angstrom Show* that your father taught you Latin. Please prove to me now that you were telling the truth. Believe me, this is very important."

With a shrug, Felix spoke off the top of his head. He said the general's name was odd because "Manes" meant "family spirits" in Latin. He then described his situation, how his father was dead, his mother was off-world, and their domestic system had been disconnected. He would have added more had the general not held up a finger.

"Thank you, that's enough," he said. "Well, Professor?"

"It is remarkable," the old man spoke in a squeaky voice, as if he hadn't practised speaking in a long, long while. "This lad's Latin is superb. His grammar's perfect, his vocabulary's rich, and he speaks without any hesitation whatsoever. My boy, I do congratulate you."

"Could he get the job done?" the general demanded.

"In my opinion, yes," the professor answered.

"Excellent. Thank you very much, Professor."

By now Felix was doubly confused. Before he could get a word out, however, the general steered him to an alcove and sat him next to Carolyn. At the same time he produced a small box from his pocket that contained a narrow hole in its side. He asked Felix to place his index finger in its hollows.

"You're about to visit a highly classified facility," he revealed. "No one can know about the secret it contains, because in the wrong hands it could lead to disaster."

"And this box …?"

"You've just sworn an oath that you'll reveal nothing about the things you're going to see. If you disclose the smallest detail to any unauthorized person, I will see to it you end up in a very dark corner of our solar system."

"I understand. I'll keep this secret to myself."

"In that case," the general said, "please secure your g-force pods."

Without further ado, the general walked to the front of the ship. Like Carolyn, Felix closed the membrane on his pod: as soon as he had, the fusion thrusters ignited and the craft leapt forward at an impressive speed.

"Where are we going?" Felix asked, over the pod's speaker.

"You'll find out soon," Carolyn said. "I'm glad you passed the Latin test. Would you believe I'd never heard of Latin until my dad found out about your story on *The Angstrom Show*?"

"*The Angstrom Show*? Is that why I'm here?"

When Carolyn didn't answer, Felix engaged the craft's external monitor. A screen came to life and revealed a view of the globe. He had to shake his head in wonder: its surface was so beautiful, with its sweeping curves and mix of luscious colours. At the same time, against the empty backdrop of space, the earth seemed ridiculous and puny-looking. When one pondered the world in relation to the universe, did it matter humans were faced with extinction? Stars, whole galaxies, had come and gone, so what importance could events on such a crumb of a planet have?

His father came to mind. Felix could picture him standing in his garden, reading a book with heartfelt satisfaction and reveling in the sun's comforting touch. He was wrong. It was in fact the tiny things that mattered. Never mind the universe's size: it was people like his father who gave it meaning.

"Dad," he whispered.

The scene on the monitor changed abruptly and its screen showed a Class 9 station floating in the distance. Felix was impressed. Shaped like an H, it was fifteen stories high and at least a hundred metres across. Its surface was covered with solar panels, signaling equipment and powerful antennae. And despite its obvious ungainliness, the structure was almost graceful as it rotated slowly against the glittering starlight.

A panel opened on the landing port. Felix felt the mildest jolt as a sea-green beam caught hold of the ship and guided it toward the station's lowest deck — like a trout being reeled in on a fishing line. A wall of electro-magnets held the craft in place and an air lock enclosed the Medevac's door. The pods opened automatically. While Carolyn hurried off to the back of the craft, Felix stood as the general approached.

"I'm glad you're with us," he declared. "But I must remind you not to disclose any aspect of this station."

"Of course, sir."

"And now I'll escort you to someone you know."

"Someone I know? Here in outer space?"

"This way, please."

The general led him through the air lock into a hallway. The air tasted strange — as if it came from a package. Felix felt less heavy than he had on Earth and realized this was due to gravity's weaker pull. As his legs bounced upwards of their own accord, he was tempted to see how high he could jump, but this wasn't the time for any such nonsense.

They entered a small elevator. After climbing four stories, the Vacu-lift opened on a figure in a lab coat. Felix gasped when he spied the man's tidy features.

"Dr. Lee!" he cried. "Why are you here?"

"Hello," the doctor replied, shaking his hand. "I'm afraid I owe you an apology, Felix. I was wrong to doubt you. It turns out you were right about everything."

"You mean...?"

"Aceticus's virus is the same one that is threatening to destroy us."

"I'm glad." Felix smiled. "I mean, I'm happy you believe me."

"And it appears," Dr. Lee continued, leading Felix and the general down a maze-like corridor, "that the *lupus ridens* is a genuine flower...."

"Then all we have to do —" Felix cried.

"Not so fast," the doctor cautioned him. "It isn't so easy."

By now they'd reached an imposing metal door that was equipped with several security scans as well as BISDMs to prevent unwanted "guests" from entering. Stepping ahead of the doctor and Felix, General Manes placed his hand on a scanner and spoke his name and title aloud: "General Isaiah Manes, commander of the Temporal Projection Matrix." Instantly, the metal door slid open.

Felix followed the men across the threshold. The sight that greeted him took his breath away.

The room he'd entered was the size of a large stadium. The floors extended the width of the station and from the floor to the ceiling was a height of six stories. In the middle of this cavern stood a shining dome — it was twelve feet high, completely transparent, and contained coloured gases spiralling about its centre. Encircling the sphere was a totalium pipe a metre wide and hooked up to an array of oscilloscopes and signallers. The space outside the sphere was packed with processors, channelers, and flashing consoles, all of them positioned round a house-sized mainframe whose interior contained a colorless plasma. This substance was hypnotic as it swirled in the most complicated patterns.

"What am I looking at?" Felix finally whispered.

"Believe it or not," the general said, "you're looking at a transportation device."

"Transportation to where?" Felix asked.

"We'll answer that soon," Dr. Lee broke in. "Let's talk about our problem first. As far as we can tell, the *lupus ridens* hasn't been seen on earth for five hundred years."

"You mean it's extinct?"

"Exactly. And because we don't know its structure, it can't be replicated."

"So we're back where we started," Felix wailed. "Aceticus is useless...."

"That's not quite true," the general mused.

"Tell me," Dr. Lee inquired, "have you studied Clavius's particle theories?"

"Just recently, yes, but I don't see ..."

"Think. What do they imply?"

"That some particles travel faster than the speed of light."

"And ...?"

"Well, in theory, that their time coefficient can be 'bent' at will."

"Precisely," the general and doctor spoke together.

"Wait, you don't mean ...?"

"That's precisely what we mean," Dr. Lee said with emphasis. "This equipment can transport people back in time. In point of fact, we wish you to travel to 71 BC when we know for certain the *lupus ridens* still existed."

Felix almost laughed. These people were talking gibberish. The past was gone, over and done with. Aceticus, Spartacus, Marcus Crassus — these figures had been dust for two thousand years and any attempt to visit them would be like attempting to bring the dead back to life.

But Dr. Lee was talking. He was saying the TPM was like a Dispersion Portal, only in addition to mere spatial coordinates, the passenger would enter a precise date as well, past, present, or future.

He also explained how they knew the TPM was functional. One month before the virus erupted, a rat had been placed in the TPM and the coordinates set for London in 1665. Before entering the device the rat had been healthy; upon emerging it was carrying the bubonic plague. There was only one possible explanation: because the plague had existed in seventeenth-century London, the rat had been projected back in time.

"If we can send a rat," Dr. Lee concluded, "we can send a human being as well, although we haven't actually done this yet."

"But ... why me?" Felix gasped.

"Two reasons," the general broke in. "First, it requires too much power to send an adult back. The TPM can handle a separate mass of maximum seventy kilograms."

"More important," Dr. Lee continued, "your Latin is excellent and you can speak to the locals."

"Why not send someone with an auto-translator?"

"Impossible!" Dr. Lee exclaimed. "The TPM can't handle metal or plastic. These substances would reflect the high-speed particles and trigger a thermonuclear explosion. If you agree to this mission, your equipment will be minimal."

"Normally we wouldn't ask you to run such risks," the general said, "but frankly, we're desperate. We're far from discovering a cure for the virus, and it's just a matter of time before everyone comes down with the plague. If you don't find this flower, and I mean *soon*, as a species, we will vanish from the face of the earth."

"The mission should be simple," Dr. Lee added. "We'll send you to a temple near Panarium — that's the town Aceticus mentions in his book — you'll venture outside, find the *lupus ridens*, hurry to a portal and return to the present."

"And you won't be alone," the general declared, "My daughter Carolyn will tag along. She doesn't speak Latin but she has certain ... skills."

"When would I leave?" Felix asked.

"Our device is powered by the sun," the doctor answered. "As temporal projection requires vast quantities of power, it must occur when the sun is at an angle of optimum impact. This will happen in twelve hours and eighteen minutes."

"Will you help us, Felix?" the general pleaded.

Aware he had no choice in the matter, Felix nodded his assent.

Chapter Six

The deadline was looming. General Manes was giving the TPM a last inspection; Dr. Lee was prepping medications in a lab; and the professor was looking after "travel arrangements." Because Carolyn had vanished without explanation, Felix was left to wander the station on his own.

As he walked about aimlessly, his thoughts turned to their mission. How much danger lay ahead of them? Would the TPM roast them to cinders? If they reached the past, would they make it back alive? Most important, would they find the *lupus ridens*? Billions of people depended on their efforts, yet their chances of success were just about zero.

To distract himself from these depressing thoughts,

Felix paused before a large, sliding door. From behind it there came the sound of ... cracking, followed by the pattering of feet. Curious, he opened the door and walked onto a "halo" court.

"Duck!" Carolyn cried.

Instinctively he dropped to his knees and a cringed as a "halo" ball whistled past him. Rubberized, three inches wide and containing circuitry at its core, it was programmed to "attack" any figure in the vicinity. The purpose of the game was to avoid the ball by bouncing off the padded walls and employing a series of complex gymnastics. Felix was pretty good at the game and could usually last well over a minute. But that was nothing compared to Carolyn's performance.

Instead of one ball, she had five in play. Each was set on maximum speed. The game should have been impossible, but Carolyn was dodging all five "halos" with ease, by contorting her limbs, climbing the walls and performing flips, cartwheels, and jumps — twice she leapt eight feet in the air. When she scaled one wall, dropped to the mat, rolled across the room and hopped to her feet, Felix raised a hand in disbelief. His gesture caused two balls to attack.

"Ow!"

"Stop!" Carolyn yelled. The halos fell to the mat.

"Are you okay?" she panted. She was dressed in a Zylex suit whose light green shimmer matched her eye colouring.

"I'm fine," Felix replied, massaging his arm. "Those balls pack a wallop."

"Personally, I find them slow for my taste."

"Have you undergone alpha-wave adjustment?"

"Of course. How else do you think I could move so quickly?"

"And did I see signs of combat training …?"

"I've mastered fifteen martial arts."

She said this matter-of-factly, as if her skills were commonplace. Felix had more questions to ask, but a voice addressed them on the room's intercom.

"Felix and Carolyn," Doctor Lee spoke up. "Could you come to my office? We have some details to go over."

"We're on our way," Carolyn replied, stepping to the exit. As she crossed the threshold, she yelled, "Attack!" Instantly the balls came alive and, if Felix hadn't leaped outside, they would have pummeled him senseless. Carolyn smirked.

A minute later they joined the doctor. A quiet man by nature — his ERR only heightened his shyness — he led them over to two "treatment" stations. As soon as they were seated, their blood chemistry was scanned. A robotic arm with needles appeared and injected them a dozen times over — with anti-viral compounds, blood-coagulants, vitamin supplements and other chemical "boosters."

With these meds dispensed, they followed the doctor to a glassed-in cubicle. At his command, three chairs rose up from the floor. And then a glowing, twelve-inch sphere rolled beside them and floated in the air until it reached eye level.

"Italy, 71 BC," the doctor announced.

The sphere projected a 3D map, which filled the room. Felix recognized Italy's boot-shaped outline; but instead of the Common Speak names for its cities, the ancient Latin ones appeared — Roma, Tarentum, Neapolis, and others.

"Panarium," the doctor spoke, causing the globe to project two maps this time. One showed Rome with its famous seven hills and, farther to the east, a town named Panarium. The second showed a town with the exact same name, only it was a hundred miles south of the first.

"As you can see," the doctor said, "There are two Panariums. While Aceticus is precise in most regards, he doesn't state which Panarium the flower can be found in. We'll hazard a guess and dispatch you to the one nearest Rome. If we're wrong, you'll return to us and we'll send you to the second one, or the town closest to it. Okay?"

They nodded.

"This brings us to the time portals. Temples," he called out.

Again the sphere projected a map, only this one showed most of Western Europe. Numerous points were flashing on its surface, in Italy and other countries as well.

"Each flashing point," the doctor explained, "is a temple that we know about from ancient times. Some were built after 71 BC, but that doesn't matter. We're establishing portals in each of these temples — including the one Mr. Taylor discovered. The second Panarium doesn't contain any temple — that's why we're sending you to the one near Rome — but there are temples not too far from it, in Paestum or Pompeii. The point is, once you enter any temple's inner recess, the portal will deposit you here."

"But can't anyone be transported?" Felix asked. "What will stop some Roman from being whisked to the present?"

"We have programmed bio-protocols in your DNA. Only you will be able to move through the portals."

"How long will the portal stay open?" Carolyn asked. "Will we be working against time?"

"No. The portal has a half-life of two hundred years. And if it's covered over, I mean, if it isn't exposed to the elements, its "charge" could last indefinitely. Now do you see that blip in the Panarium near Rome? That's your point of entry. It is a temple of Minerva — the goddess of wisdom. Let's hope her wisdom rubs off on us."

Again they nodded. Because the doctor had "unplug-ged" the sphere, they assumed he was done with them and rose from their seats. But he motioned them to sit again, as his face assumed a grim expression.

"Have you heard about the butterfly effect?" he asked.

"I have," Carolyn volunteered. "It's the change you can trigger in the present or future by travelling back in time and altering events. So if you killed my great-great-grandfather, say, his descendants would vanish, includ-ing me and my father."

"That's right," the doctor said, nodding. "Now, our calculations tell us that you can change our present only if you harm someone or reveal some hidden aspect of the future — if you teach them about nuclear fission, for example. That is why, no matter what, you will not kill or injure anyone, even as a matter of self-defence. And you must not talk in any way about our future. The survival of our world depends upon your vigilance. Do you understand?"

The doctor glared at them. Understanding the grav-ity of his words, they promised to follow his instruc-tions exactly.

"In that case," he concluded, "I wish you both the best of luck."

The trio stood. Shaking hands with them, the doctor revealed that the professor was in a room across the hall where he would provide them with some "travel" information. Without another word, he exited the cubicle and joined the general in his inspection of the TPM.

Carolyn and Felix crossed the hall and, sure enough, found the professor seated in a cubicle. In front of him were two bundles of cloth. Surrounding him were several stacks of books, many of them with Latin titles. At the sight of these, Felix grinned: books always made him feel optimistic.

And then there was the professor himself. He was peculiar-looking. He was bald and wrinkled and frail and stooped over: clearly he had rejected all revitalizing treatments. To judge by his vivid and lively expression, he had also turned his back on ERR. Finally, his glasses were so thick and clumsy — the frames kept slipping off the bridge of his nose — that they gave him a decidedly comical air. There was nothing comical about his gaze, however: his eyes radiated a vast intelligence.

"All right," he began, motioning them to sit. "Our first task is to determine who you are. In the unlikely event you get stranded in the past, the ancients you encounter will ask where you're from."

"*Tis pothen eis andron,*" Felix murmured.

"Precisely!" the professor declared with delight, "I didn't know you were trained in Greek! My, my, you are full of surprises."

"What did you just say?" Carolyn demanded.

"It comes from a poem called *The Odyssey*," Felix said. "It means 'Who are you and where do you come from?'"

Chuckling still, the professor said the locals would ask about their Common Speak and why Carolyn didn't know any Latin. They would inquire about their status too — were they *peregrini* (foreigners), slaves, or citizens? Finally, their relationship would stir their curiosity, as well as the fact that they were travelling solo.

"What do you propose?" Felix asked.

"First," the professor said, "you are brother and sister."

"They won't believe it," Carolyn snapped. "We don't look at all alike."

The professor laughed. "That's not quite true. Both of you are tall, fair-complexioned, and blue-eyed. The Romans will assume you're from the north; indeed, you'll claim to come from Prytan — that is, modern-day Britain — and say you are descended from a line of Druids."

"What's a Druid?" Carolyn asked, with a touch of impatience.

Felix told her Druids were leaders among the ancient Celts — he didn't dare mention they were priests as well because Carolyn would resent this reference to religion.

"Your father, Felix," the professor pressed on, "has dispatched you to learn the Romans' customs. You have spent three years with Sextus Pullius Aceticus who happens to live in Cisalpine Gaul — northern Italy, of course. This is where you learned your excellent Latin. Indeed, you have proven such an adept student that Aceticus has adopted you and rendered you a citizen."

"What about me?" Carolyn asked.

"Ah yes. Your father died recently — the Druid and not the general — and that is why you have joined your brother. In your father's absence, he leads the family. And before returning to Prytan, to become head Druid, Felix has decided to take a tour of Rome. That's not a bad biography, if I say so myself."

Felix was impressed. This story would account for their overall strangeness and grant them a certain freedom of movement. He was pleased, too, that his "adoptive father" was the author who had led them to the *lupus ridens.*

"Now then," the professor went on, pointing to the two bundles before him, "after consulting my books, I have created two tunics for you — with help from an automated loom, of course. You have also been given a *toga virilis*, Felix, which will mark you off as a Roman *civis.*"

"Do I get a toga?" Carolyn asked, inspecting her clothes with a hint of suspicion.

"Women don't wear togas," the professor replied. "And that's why I have provided you with a *palla*, or cloak. You'll also find *calcei*, or leather sandals. As far as *indumenta*, or undergarments are concerned, we'll dispense with the *licium*, an uncomfortable loincloth, and you'll wear our modern products instead. If you're asked about these, you'll say they are worn in Prytan."

"Why do I smell cinnamon?" Felix asked. He was sniffing a leather pouch.

With an elfish smile, the professor explained he'd had a stroke of genius. If the pair of them got delayed in the past, they would need some type of currency. Gold was impossible — the TPM would reject it — so something else would have to serve in its place.

"Why cinnamon?" Carolyn asked.

"Because back then cinnamon was very precious. A single pinch will buy you a bed for the night."

Rising from his seat, he said they should go to their quarters and try their outfits on; quickly, too, as they would be leaving soon. He removed his glasses and polished the lenses, resembling a mole as he eyed them both.

"I envy you," he said. "To think that you will escape our modern machines to gaze upon the Romans sends shivers up my spine. But be very careful. These people are as brutal as they are civilized."

The pair nodded. Shaking hands with him, they took their bundles and left the room. As they headed toward two changing rooms, both were thinking the moment of truth was approaching. They were wondering, too, if

they would get along: Carolyn found Felix odd, while
Felix found Carolyn brash and pushy. On the other hand,
they were glad they wouldn't be travelling solo.

In his room, Felix stripped down to his Protek under-
wear and reached for the tunic, which was two linen
squares sewn simply together, with two rough holes for
his arms and head. Pulling on the garment, he bunched
its folds around his waist and tied these in place with a
thin, leather strap. His feet groped for the sandals, which
fitted him well — instead of buckles, there were straps
that he could tighten at will. That left him with the toga.

He was acquainted with togas because he had woven
one once, just to see what the effect would be. It was
two metres long and a metre wide, with three straight
sides and a semi-circular one. The trick was to secure
one end to the shoulder and wrap its length maybe twice
around the waist, draping the loose end in the crook
of one's arm. It took him half-a-dozen attempts before
he felt its folds were decently arranged. As an article of
dress it was ridiculous and cumbersome.

He had barely finished dressing when a knock rang out.
A moment later, General Manes walked into the room.

"Hello, sir," Felix spoke. "What do you think? Does
the toga suit me?"

"Very much so," the general replied, attempting a
smile but barely succeeding.

"Is it time?"

"I'm afraid so. Carolyn is waiting at the TPM and I decided to escort you myself."

"I see. That's kind of you."

Following the general, Felix stepped into the hallway, his movements uncertain because the toga kept slipping. As they proceeded to the Vacu-lift, he could sense the general had something to say, but that he wasn't sure how to broach the subject.

"Is something on your mind, sir?" he prodded him.

"You're intuitive," the general said with approval. "That's one advantage of being ERR-free. I'm worried about my daughter, of course. Since her mother's death four years ago, she is all I've got. She means the moon and sun to me."

"I'll do my best to keep her safe," Felix promised. "Although she seems pretty good at looking after herself."

"True enough," the general agreed, with the tiniest smile. A grimmer expression quickly returned, "More to the point, the news from earth is very worrying. The infection rate stands at sixty-eight percent — it has increased by ten percent these last six hours. Not too many victims have died, but that will change within a week at most. I don't mean to pressure you, son, but you've got to find that flower. Otherwise ..." The general left this sentence hanging.

There was nothing else to say. Felix accompanied General Manes the rest of the way in silence.

A mere two minutes later, he and Carolyn were poised in front of the TPM. He felt like a sailor on the shore of the sea: on one side was the tranquil present; ahead was the future's choppy expanse.

Carolyn stood behind him. He could see her reflected in the TPM's dome: her *palla* was a perfect fit and she was utterly composed: she reminded him of the goddess Diana. Her father was watching from a distant console, with the same detachment and self-control. He was possibly about to kill his child, but his gaze was unwavering and his features calm. Even as he envied them their ERR, Felix suspected that they'd been robbed of something crucial.

A flashing light disrupted these thoughts. The TPM was primed and it was time to enter. With nods to the general, doctor, and professor, Felix inhaled deeply and crossed the threshold. His nose was itchy and wanted scratching but even as he raised his finger, a light burst forth and an electrical surge ripped through him.

In the hollows of the TPM, Felix Taylor was no longer to be seen.

Chapter Seven

Teleportation was usually a humdrum affair. The process was so blindingly fast that the passenger hadn't time to feel his atoms dissolve, travel through space, and reassemble elsewhere. But Dispersion Portals were one thing, the TPM was something different.

While the machine's operations were lightning-fast, they seemed to transpire in slow motion. As a result, Felix saw his surroundings "melt" into a single point, the TPM, the space station, the earth, the sun, the solar system, and Milky Way. A storm of sound engulfed him, a mix of roars, cries, laughter, and eruptions, as worlds were born and destroyed in an instant, coming to be and expiring in a flash, like an infant's puny wail of frustration. A million points of light tore at his "fabric" and

spread it over an impossibly great distance, kilometres
— no — *light years* in length: his limbs, his torso, his
head ran on and on, all connected to each other still,
but stretched like taffy over time and space. His senses
were intact and he controlled his movements, even as
a force ushered him forward, along a path of light that
was wobbling like jelly. His index finger was still in front
of his nose and was long enough to reach the sun as well
as every other star at large.

And then it was over. Like a stretched elastic snapping back to normal, his atoms reassembled in the blink
of an eye. He inhaled deeply, coughed once or twice,
and felt his limbs over to check that he was ... solid.

It was dark around him. Before he could puzzle his
surroundings out, he was struck from behind. Stumbling forward, he bumped into a smooth, hard surface.
What ...?

"Felix?" Carolyn gasped. "Where are you?"

He started at the sound of her voice, and realized
just as quickly he was glad to hear it. Reassuring her
he was there, he again looked his surroundings over. By
now his eyes were adjusting to the dark and the object
in front of him was coming into focus. It was a statue as
far as he could tell, a female with a helmet and.... His
body tingled.

"Is that what we're looking for?" Carolyn asked.

"Yes," Felix croaked. "It's a statue of Minerva."

"The Roman goddess of wisdom," she said.

"We're in a *cella*," Felix said, ignoring the scorn in her voice. "That's the inner room of a Roman temple and the place where the statue of the god is stored."

"So we've arrived."

"It looks that way. Let's get out of here. Do you see a door?"

They glanced around. There. Five metres in front of them was a square outline of light. They moved toward it cautiously and worked the heavy planking open. Scouring sunlight poured into the room.

Blinking hard, they surveyed their surroundings. Before them was a stylobate or elongated floor that carried lines of marble columns. Above them was the architrave, or beams, that supported the temple's elaborate frieze: these marble blocks were handsomely carved and depicted myths from the life of Minerva. Felix wanted to study them, but a shove from Carolyn brought him to his senses. There was work to be done. Inching forward, they reached the stylobate's end and a flight of marble stairs. Both of them gasped.

The temple stood on a hill. Below them was a series of fields that rolled on forever, bursting with wheat and other produce. Far off in the distance, on the edge of the horizon, stood a line of intoxicating blue: the sea.

A golden sun illuminated this landscape, its rays teasing the odd meandering cloud.

Neither Felix nor Carolyn could speak. While comfortable, their world was overcrowded. There were very few open areas left, where tracts of land greeted the eye and nature could assert itself so freely. Even the sun and sky were different, were richer in tone, more deeply hued, because they weren't subject yet to human control.

Human control. A mile to their right stood a square-shaped town with a collection of houses and buildings at its centre. It was surrounded by a wall, with a gate on each side, through which multitudes of people were exiting and entering. An army had pitched its camp outside the town and the locals were anxious to trade with the soldiers. Lots of men were riding about on horses. Felix and Carolyn stood agog: horses were very rare in their world and found in only three or four zoos.

"Are we here," Carolyn whispered, "or are we part of some virtual reality?"

Before Felix could speak, a voice called to them.

"Come away from there, you two!"

Felix glanced down. A man in a tunic was glaring up at them. He was short and wiry and was surrounded by goats — animals Felix had never seen in the flesh. More to the point, the man was addressing them in Latin.

"Don't stand there like two dolts! Come away from there!"

"What's he saying?" Carolyn asked.

"He wants us to come down. Look around for a field with flowers. Quickly. This guy is just about ready to explode. "

Felix was right. The man was yelling and gesturing at the pair. Other people were gathering now, lured by the commotion. All of them were yelling as well.

"I can't see any flowers," Carolyn said. "What now?"

"We'll have to search for it the hard way."

"Maybe we're in the wrong Panarium."

"We can't know that for sure. Let's check things out."

Felix descended the stairs, his gait somewhat awkward because his toga kept slipping. Carolyn followed, muttering to herself. The crowd confronted them at the foot of the hill.

"Explain yourself!" the first man cried. His face was burned a chestnut brown and he was missing two fingers.

"The goddess is moody," a woman added. She was dressed in a tunic that had been patched all over, two incisors were missing, and she had a bad rash.

"You're not from here!" a third person yelled, brandishing a hoe.

"That is so," Felix replied, anxious to test his Latin on a band of native speakers. "We're priests from Prytan and wished to visit your goddess. We meant no harm."

The crowd's mood underwent a sudden reversal. From hostile and suspicious, they became friendly and servile. They had noticed how well-dressed their visitors were, how their skin was fair, and their teeth white and even. They were clearly well connected, to a senator perhaps. And they were priests! Maybe they would bring the town good luck.

"Is this Panarium?" Felix asked, addressing the first man.

"Yes, *amice*. It is the finest town in Italy, I daresay."

"Do you know a farmer named Balbus?"

"No, *adulescens*. I have never heard of Balbus. But there are numerous households in this region, and our prefect may be acquainted with this person."

"Many thanks. You have been most helpful."

"The pleasure is mine, *domine*."

"*Curate ut valeatis.*"

"*Valete*, both of you."

Motioning to Carolyn, Felix led her down a narrow road toward the town's sturdy ramparts. As they walked, he summarized his exchange with the crowd and suggested that they were best off consulting the prefect.

"I still say we're in the wrong town," she maintained.

"Maybe, but let's make sure."

They continued along the road in silence. While Felix felt vaguely pleased with himself — he hadn't known how a Roman would respond to his Latin — Carolyn was irritable. Her lack of language frustrated her, and their surroundings were more alien than she had expected.

"Look at this road," she finally spoke, after stubbing her toe for the fifteenth time, "It's riddled with potholes."

"It's a secondary road, a *via glarea*," Felix answered. "But in the eyes of the ancients, even a road like this is a marvel."

"There are no lights. Imagine walking it at night."

"You wouldn't. Unless there were a full moon and you were properly armed."

"And look at these fields. They're empty. What's the use of wasting land?"

"It's not being wasted. The Romans don't synthesize their food. This wheat you see will be turned into bread."

"It's so ... so ... primitive," she observed. "Although the effect is very pretty."

By now they had reached Panarium's outskirts. The area was packed with legionnaires and merchants and market stalls full of various wares. Flies were swarming everywhere, and the gnarled and unhygienic crowd kept fingering the produce, even as the merchants told them to keep their filthy hands to themselves. Children had a free run of the place, and there were dogs everywhere, on the lookout for scraps. A withered man was playing a pipe, while a knot of soldiers, reeling with drink, danced to his plaintive tune.

"This place is unbelievable," Carolyn observed.

"Let me ask someone where we can find the town prefect."

Felix approached a stall that contained plates of pastry — grainy cakes of dough that were swimming in oil. He had to brush a dozen flies from his face as he confronted the owner, a big-headed man with piercing black eyes.

"What can I do for you, *adulescens*?"

"Where can I find the prefect, please?"

"Why do you want the prefect?"

"I'm looking for a farmer named Balbus and ..."

"Balbus? I've never heard of him. Hey!" he called to several passersby. "Do you know a farmer named Balbus? Marcus? Octavia?"

A knot of people quickly formed. Again Felix couldn't help but notice how tough they seemed, how gnarled and short and badly bruised by life. One had a facial scar, another an arm that was sorely misshapen, and a third was missing his right leg altogether. Glancing

Felix over, they said no farmer named Balbus lived in the region. Felix was about to grimace in frustration when a boy came running up to his side. He was eight years old and cradling a hen — again this was an animal that was rarely seen in modern times.

"I know a Balbus," he piped up. "He lives in my hometown, which is a five-day walk from here."

"Then he can't be the right Balbus, can he?" the pastry man sneered.

"But this Balbus is famous," the boy persisted, "Instead of grain, his land is choked with flowers, that's how much the gods detest him."

"That *is* the Balbus I'm looking for!" Felix felt a surge of excitement. "Where are you from?"

"I'm from a hamlet called Canepria. It is one of several *viculi* that lie close together.... Ah! I understand!" the boy proclaimed. "A second Panarium lies three miles north of us. That's the place you're after, and not this *oppidum* here."

He began to laugh at Felix's mistake, as did the rest of the group. But the chicken in his arms took fright at this clamour, beat its wings vigorously, and escaped his arms. With a cry of anguish the boy set off in pursuit. Laughing still, the crowd went about their business.

"What a bumpkin that boy is," the pastry man chuckled. "Although I feel bad for his family. They fled here to escape Spartacus's army and have lost their farm and all of their possessions...."

Felix was only half listening. He was explaining to Carolyn what the boy had said, and how they had in fact selected the wrong Panarium. Both agreed that they should return to the temple, and were turning to leave when the man snatched Felix's arm.

"One moment," he growled, "Is that how you repay a favour? I helped you find that farmer Balbus, and the least you can do is buy a piece of my pastry. Your wife is thin and could use some fattening up."

"She's my sister," Felix replied. "But you're right. A thousand pardons. We'll take two servings of your pastry, *optime*."

"That's more like it. I made them fresh this morning and they are full of honey. And at ten *sesterces* they are an excellent bargain...."

"I can't pay in cash." Felix was loosening the string on his pouch.

"You have no cash?" the owner groaned, "So what will you give me...?"

"*Cinnamomum*," Felix said, holding out a large pinch of the spice. With a look of incredulity, the vendor brought his nose to Felix's fingers.

"*Cinnamomum*! I don't believe ...? Here. Take as much pastry as you want!"

"Two pieces are enough." Felix laughed, sprinkling the powder onto the stall's pitted counter. That said, he and Carolyn stepped away. The vendor was too excited to notice: he was gathering the spice and sniffing it ecstatically.

Nibbling on the pastry, they hatched a simple plan. Now that they knew where to find the *lupus ridens*, they would return to their present and travel to the right Panarium. Balbus would be easy to track down — he seemed to be well known in the region — and once they had the *lupus ridens*, their mission would be over. All in all it seemed very straightforward. Felix was going to say as much, when someone seized him from behind.

"Hey!" he cried, as he was shoved into a space behind an empty stall. Carolyn was being similarly handled.

"*Tace, amice,*" one man spoke. He was powerfully built, burned black by the sun, and had a menacing, lopsided grin. His companions had the same hardened appearance. Felix saw that they were dressed in identical *lacernae*, short cloaks fastened with a clasp at the shoulder, and grasped that they were part of the visiting army.

"Can we help you?" he asked.

"As a matter of fact, you can. Hand us the *cinnamomum* and we'll leave you alone."

"What do they want?" Carolyn asked.

"It's the cinnamon. They saw it when I paid for the pastry. I'll give it to them...."

"You can't. It could easily trigger a butterfly effect. With wealth like that, these men could alter the future."

"You're right. What do you suggest ...?"

"Enough gibberish!" the leader barked. "Hand the loot over!"

"I'm sorry," Felix said. "I can't."

"I'm not asking," the man growled, pulling a dagger from his tunic. It was sharp and looked like it had been used before. "Give it to me now or ..."

By the time he looked behind him, Carolyn had knocked down all his friends, tempering her blows so she would only bruise them. With movements too fast for the eye to follow, she grabbed the dagger from the leader's hand. The man cursed and threw a punch, but she ducked it easily and brought him to his knees.

"Tell them to leave," she said.

Before Felix could translate, the men were up again and bent on violence. Three of them had daggers now and were closing in on Carolyn. Felix raised his fists, but she needed no assistance. Effortlessly, she had them on the ground again, with no damage afflicted but for minor aches and sprains. Full with rage, the men were going to rush her a third time. Before they could, a voice rang out.

"That's enough! Attention, all of you!"

Felix glanced around. Other troops had gathered without his noticing, as well as a man who was mounted on a charger. His clothing marked him out as a general: he was wearing a breastplate, a leather kilt, and a blood-red cloak that reached his calves. Felix started. He recognized this man. He'd seen pictures of his bust before and … yes! As incredible as it seemed, he was poised before Pompey the Great, one of Rome's greatest leaders.

"Explain yourselves!" Pompey was directing his soldiers.

"We were having a joke, *dux*." the leader spoke, "We intended no harm."

"Is that true?" Pompey asked Carolyn. The epitome of calm when she'd been fighting, she looked lost and confused when the general addressed her.

"It is true, *dux*," Felix volunteered, aware that if he told the truth, the soldiers would be flogged and their wounds might lead to a butterfly effect, "They meant no harm."

"Who are you?" Pompey demanded, frowning at Felix's accent. "And why does this girl not speak for herself? She fights for herself," he added, with a look of approval.

"She speaks no Latin, *dux*. And my name is Felix Aceticus, son of the Druid Belenus from Prytan, and adopted son of Sextus Pullius Aceticus."

"You're Sextus's adopted son?" Pompey asked, smiling suddenly. "Why didn't you say so? The old bookworm is a client of mine, although it has been ages since I last saw him in Cremona. But I'm tired of talking in the open like this." He called to a servant with enormous ears. "Flaccus! See to my guests. They will come with us to Rome this afternoon."

"Very good, *dux*."

Felix wanted to say they had business to look after, but the general had already turned his back on them. His soldiers followed after him, but not before their attackers looked them over, bewildered why they'd been let off so easy. Felix was hoping that he and Carolyn might escape in this confusion and return to the temple and the TPM, but Flaccus was keeping a close eye on them.

"You heard the *dux*," he said, leading them forward. "You're coming with us."

With no choice in the matter, the pair stepped off. While Felix was thrilled at the thought of spending time with Pompey, part of him suspected that they were sticking their necks on a chopping block.

Chapter Eight

Felix rolled onto his back and exchanged stares with a ceiling. He had slept like the dead and, in his first waking moments, had trouble recollecting where he was. Wrestling back his panic, he pieced his memories together.

He was in ... Italy, 71 BC. Check.

At Pompey's prompting, his slave Flaccus had piled them into a wagon. Check.

They had travelled along the Via Nomentum to Rome, at which stage they had left the wagon and followed Pompey when he'd passed behind the Servian Walls. Check.

Inside Rome they had wandered the Via Longus, with its towering apartment blocks on either side, whose ground floors had exhibited a hive of stores, each buzzing with crowds of noisy shoppers. As they had walked between the Quirinal and Viminal hills, he'd descried the temple to Jupiter on the Capitoline's crest. Check.

At the foot of the Esquiline, Pompey had turned up a steep, winding alley. After a gruelling hike, he had led them to a spectacular *domus* on the southeast slope. Check.

Entering the house, they had been welcomed by a crowd of slaves. Advising them that dinner would be served before sunset, Flaccus had led them to separate rooms. Check.

After dismissing his slave, a Spaniard named Fuscus, Felix had washed using a pitcher of water, then stretched out on a bed and fallen asleep, overcome by the heat and the strangeness of time travel. Check.

And now Fuscus was due to arrive at any moment and conduct him to the *triclinium* where dinner would be held. Check.

He shook his head wearily. It defied belief that he was present in Republican Rome, and was rubbing shoulders with one of its most famous sons. On the one hand, he was smiling with pleasure; on the other, he was aware they had a mission to complete. Never mind his encounter with Pompey; they had to find the *lupus ridens* and …

A knock rang out and Carolyn entered.

"You look upset," Felix said.

"A slave wanted to wash me and help me dress," she complained. "Are people so helpless they can't manage these tasks for themselves?"

"We're not much different. We rely on our machines."

"Programming a machine isn't the same as bullying humans. But never mind that. Have you figured out a way to escape this place? We've got to track that flower down."

"I know. I'm hoping Pompey will escort us there himself."

He explained that, if he remembered correctly, Pompey had just returned from a campaign in Spain. Within a week, having tidied up his affairs in Rome, he would march his army south to join the struggle against Spartacus. They would proceed along the Via Appia and pass within a short distance of Panarium.

"Will he take us along?" Carolyn asked.

"We'll persuade him to. If not, we'll think of something else. In the meantime, let's try to blend in with these Romans."

He would have added more but Flaccus appeared just then to take them to dinner. Stepping into the main hall, they walked toward the rear of the *domus*. The dying sun was entering through a hole in a roof (it was called a *compluvium*) and a dozen lamps were casting light from a variety of alcoves. Three servants stood with buckets at hand, just in case a fire started.

En route to the dining room, they passed a chamber that exhibited lines of masks on its walls. The features on each were detailed and realistic, and the collection created an eerie impression, as if a multitude of spirits were watching them pass.

"Why the masks?" Carolyn whispered.

"They are portraits of Pompey's ancestors. Some go back hundreds of years."

"They're … peculiar."

"Shh. We're here."

They were standing with Flaccus at the doorway of the *triclinium*. Boisterous voices were coming from within, and a crowd of servants were streaming back and forth, carrying wine and platters of food. Two slaves seated Felix and Carolyn on stools, washed their feet, and provided them with slippers. This operation done, they were ushered forward.

They gasped at the sight before them. They were in a room whose length was twice its width and whose walls were painted a mix of cheerful colours. There were lamps everywhere, and two more servants to prevent a fire from starting. Most peculiar were the dining arrangements. Instead of a regular table and chairs, three couches had been arranged to form a square with one side missing. The space in between contained three long tables, with sufficient room for slaves to pass into the middle. And instead of sitting straight, the guests were reclining on their sides, their faces turned toward the central space. All in all, it was a cozy setup.

The diners barely noticed as Flaccus guided them to the couch on the left — by custom this was reserved for the lowest-ranking guests. They were too caught up in the conversation and, besides, two fifteen-year-old foreigners were hardly worth their notice. Felix looked round the room and almost flinched in shock. Besides Pompey, there were another five people, two of whom he recognized. Containing his excitement, he reclined beside Carolyn on the couch.

"So tell us," Pompey asked the man on his right, a sign his rank was the highest of those present, "how's the war with Spartacus going?"

"We have five legions and are assembling three more," this guest spoke crisply, holding out his goblet, which a slave filled with wine.

"Eight legions to deal with an army of slaves?" Pompey laughed.

"Your attitude explains why we've been beaten thus far. Don't underrate these slaves, Gnaeus. They are capable warriors."

"But they are slaves, nonetheless," a portly man spoke up. "Doesn't Aristotle argue that some are slaves by nature while others are born to rule?"

"With all due respect to Aristotle," the general sneered, "Spartacus fights for a most precious possession, his personal liberty. This is why his motivation is high, and why he has performed so ably. At the same time, he will learn to his discredit that it is sheer folly to defy the authority of Rome."

"Do you recognize these people?" Carolyn whispered.

"Only two besides Pompey," Felix replied, nodding his thanks as a slave handed him a goblet. "On his right is Marcus Licinius Crassus, the richest man in Rome; while the fat guy is Marcus Tullius Cicero, a very able orator."

"I don't know what they're saying, but they seem pleased with themselves."

"You're right," Felix said, discovering there was wine in his goblet. "As far as I can tell, they are all big players on the political scene. Still, if they knew what I know, they wouldn't feel so smug."

In a low voice he described how each character would meet his end. Pompey would die years later in Egypt, murdered after his defeat by Julius Caesar. Cicero would be killed by a follower of Caesar — the infamous Mark Antony. And Crassus would die in the

Syrian desert after witnessing the destruction of his accompanying army.

"It's eerie," Carolyn commented, "how you know these men's futures."

Felix was about to agree — it was strange to know how a living person would die — but their whispering had attracted the guests' attention and they were now the subject of everyone's stares. To conceal his agitation, Felix gulped his wine.

"What language are you speaking?" Cicero asked.

"It is a dialect of Celtic," Felix lied, aware that the orator couldn't tell Common Speak and Celtic apart.

"Pompey tells us that you are from Prytan," Crassus said, "and you are descended from Druids?"

"That is correct, *dux*."

"Tell us about Prytan and your people, then."

Aware that Romans were curious about the world, Felix had prepared himself in advance for this question. He briefly described the size and climate of England, as well as its tribes and religious practices, explaining how the Druids worship nature and consider fire a purifying element. As he spoke, he knew no one would challenge his account: no Roman would set foot in Prytan for at least twenty years.

"How fascinating," a man named Metellus spoke up. "It is remarkable how varied the world can be."

Crassus laughed. "How backward, too. The boy's account just goes to show that the world is waiting for the Romans to fill it."

"Perhaps Prytan will experience the force of Roman arms," Cicero agreed. "And will be fortunate enough to become a province. How does that prospect strike you, boy?"

"Perhaps it will be conquered," Felix assented, aware the emperor Claudius would turn it into a province down the road. Without considering the wisdom of the remark, he added, "But the student of history cannot fail to observe that empires eventually come to an end. Indeed, the larger their territory, the faster they contract."

The room greeted his statement with silence. Pompey was holding out his goblet but moved it suddenly when Felix spoke, causing wine to spill all over. Crassus sat upright, knocking into Metellus, who dropped a succulent slice of lamb. The other guests were murmuring aloud, shocked by Felix's observation. Sensing he had spoken out of turn, Carolyn curled into herself.

"Pompeius informs us," Cicero spoke, "that you have been adopted by Sextus Pullius Aceticus and trained in Roman customs?"

"That is correct, *magister*." Felix glanced down at his goblet. In his nervousness, he had drained its contents.

"And yet, having received such instruction, you question our supremacy?"

"I meant no offence. I was merely pointing out that empires die, like all things human. Why are Babylonia, Assyria, and Egypt no more? Because they overreached themselves and committed terrible crimes."

"Such as?" Crassus asked, his face a mix of ice and stone.

"Enslaving people is one example."

The room started speaking at once. Someone was yelling that an economy without slaves was impossible; Cicero was quoting Aristotle again, how some populations are naturally servile; while Crassus was saying it was talk like Felix's that encouraged slaves to rebel against their masters. Finally Pompey stared at Felix and demanded loudly, "Whose side are you on? Do you fight for Rome or is it Spartacus you champion?"

Felix was tipsy but realized he had gone too far. Somehow he had to fix this situation and regain these politicians' good will. He stared up at the ceiling for some inspiration, where a painting of Venus looked down at him. Venus, the goddess of love, mother of Aeneas and … Aeneas! Of course!

A moment later the crowd was amazed when Felix left his couch and stepped into the centre. He raised his arms, closed his eyes and began to recite from memory:

Arma virumque cano, Troae qui primus ab oris
Italiam fato profugus Laviniaque venit
litora — multum ille et terris iactatus et alto
vi superum, saevae memorem Iunonis ob iram,
multa quoque et bello passus, dum conderet urbem
inferretque deos Latio; genus unde Latinum
Albanique patres atque altae moenia Romae.

Felix would later translate these lines into Common
Speak for Carolyn:

I sing of weapons and the man. Fleeing Troy's
    coast
he was fated first to reach Italy and the shores
    of Lavinia,
tossed on sea and land by divine violence,
because savage Juno was ever mindful of her
    anger.
He also endured the travails of war, until he
    should found the city
and carry his gods into Latium. From him come
    the Latin tribe,
the Alban nobles and the defenses of lofty Rome.

Watching Felix, Carolyn didn't know what to think.
Part of her believed he had lost his mind; another part

admired him for his courage in confronting a throng of angry Romans; finally, part of her was full of wonder. It wasn't only that his performance was breathtaking, even though she couldn't understand a word he had spoken; it was his influence on the guests. They were staring at him in amazement. Whereas a minute earlier, Cicero had been contorted with rage, the orator was smiling and had his eyes shut tight, as if he were listening to his favourite piece of music. Crassus was waving his hand to Felix's chanting, while Pompey, the battle-hardened general, had *tears* stealing from his eyes!

Regaining his composure, Felix finished his recital and lowered his arm.

"I hope you accept these lines of verse," he spoke, "as an apology for my inopportune remarks."

"How is it," Cicero finally spoke, "that a native son of Prytan could compose the finest Latin verse I've ever heard?"

"The gods are speaking through this boy," Metellus agreed.

"He has breathed such honey from his lips," Crassus cried, "that he has more than made up for his earlier poison."

"Be seated," Pompey finally spoke, holding his goblet up in Felix's honour. "Adopted son of Aceticus, never mind your unconventional views. I am honoured that you are here beneath my roof. Tomorrow we shall attend a *munus* and I shall grant you any wish you desire. And now, back to our feast."

Bowing low, Felix retreated to the couch. Reclining next to Carolyn, he grabbed her goblet and drained it of its water. Her face was full of questions, so he explained that Romans were crazy about poetry and he had recited a few verses from the greatest poet of them all, Publius Vergilius Maro.

"Of course," he added with a grin, "his *Aeneid* won't appear for fifty years."

He then said that Pompey had promised to grant him a favour. Assuming the general was heading south with his troops, he would ask his permission to accompany the army as far as Panarium. Although they would have to attend a *munus* first.

"What's a *munus*?"

Instead of answering, Felix helped himself to some chicken. With a sour look he ripped apart the bones and sunk his teeth into the tender flesh.

Chapter Nine

A blast of trumpets split the air and seemed to shake all of Felix's bones. He was sitting in a front row of the Circus Maximus, the city's largest venue for mass entertainment, and felt small in a crowd of some thirty thousand people. Everyone was in excellent spirits: the *munus* would be starting soon and promised to be magnificent. For his part, he felt sick to his stomach.

Not that the morning hadn't had its moments. After breakfast, he and Carolyn had joined Pompey on a stroll through the city. For several hours they had toured numerous districts, being careful not to approach a line of chalk-white markers. When Carolyn had asked why Pompey was avoiding this boundary, Felix had told her it was something called the *Pomerium* and marked the original outline of Rome: once a general crossed it, he would be stripped of his office.

They had taken in a multitude of sights from a distance. These had included a host of temples, shops, public buildings, and, visible on the Capitoline, the Tarpeian Rock: it was from here that criminals were thrown to their deaths. After lunch in a *taberna*, they had walked along the Via Tuscus, past the Forum Boarium (or cattle market), and into the vast circus itself, where they'd been sitting for the last half hour.

It would have been glorious had they not been faced with a *munus*.

Another clarion call erupted, this one more piercing than the first. When its final note died, Pompey climbed to his feet and waved regally to the crowd around him. Nearby spectators yelled his name, then the people beside them picked up the cry, and so the roar spread from tier to tier, until the entire building quaked with shouts of "Pompey! Pompey!" He was nodding, waving, and perspiring slightly — and clearly enjoying this thunderous applause. And why not, Felix thought. Wasn't he footing the bill for this show, to express his thanks for his triumphs in Spain?

"Pompey! *Imperator*!" the mob kept yelling, and Pompey grinned at this title of acclaim. *Imperator*, conqueror, the title pleased him greatly. But even as he stood there, vigorous and full of life, Felix couldn't help but shudder. In contrast to this triumph, the hero would die a lonely death years later, stabbed in the back and swiftly beheaded....

"If they're happy now," he commented, "just wait until the show begins."

"I'm sure it will be impressive," Felix said, suppressing his knowledge of the general's fate. "But can I remind you of your promise at dinner last night?"

The general laughed. "That depends on what I promised."

"You said you would reward me."

"I remember," he nodded, with a serious expression. "What would you like?"

"We would like to join you when you march south with your troops."

"You could ask for gold," Pompey said. "but prefer to visit a war zone?" He laughed again.

"I have my reasons. Anyway, that is what I wish."

Saying he would mull it over, the general chatted with Crassus, who was sitting one seat over. Felix told Carolyn that he had asked Pompey his favour.

"Good. This place is maddening," she growled. "No one has undergone ERR and the crowd seems unstable and capable of anything."

"You're not used to humans in their natural state."

"… And then there are the temples you keep pointing out, not to mention statues of their so-called gods. These people rule the world and should have faith in their reason; instead they're hysterical and superstitious." She shuddered with contempt.

"That's because life is uncertain — they could die of disease or war or famine. Their faith in gods allows them to think the world is stable and their lives are worth living."

"But it's so … ridiculous. I'll bet these people rob for their gods, kill for them, and take slaves for them. I haven't studied history like you, but I know about the wars in the twenty-first century, and how they erupted because of religion.…"

"Religion has been toxic," Felix agreed. "But at the same time it's been a crucial stage in our development, introducing us to justice and the sanctity of life. My father often argued that without religion, our species would never have survived its childhood."

This mention of his father was like picking at a scab. He might have started brooding on his loss had a trumpet blast not sounded and roused the crowd to their feet. A band of men were entering the circus. They were armed but could not be confused with soldiers. Instead, Felix recognized the stock gladiator types. There was the *retiarius*, who was armed with a net and a vicious-looking trident; the *murmillo*, with his crested helmet and a long, straight blade; the *hoplomachus*, with his shield and massive spear; and the *thraex*, who carried a sword that was lethally curved at its tip.

"What's all this?" Carolyn asked.

"You won't want to watch," Felix warned her.

"Why? The crowd seems very excited."

At the sound of yet another trumpet call, the gladiators marched to one side, leaving two men behind to fight each other, a *murmillo* and a *hoplomachus*. The latter looked young, maybe twenty years old, and was lean and wiry; his opponent was older — his hair was grey — yet was muscular and vastly experienced (or so his many scars suggested). The pair faced Pompey, their arms upraised in a salute. Together they chanted, *"Ave Imperator, morituri te salutamus"* ("Hail general, we about to die salute you"). Pompey nodded and signalled them to begin.

The pair drew apart, crouched low and circled each other, like two dogs warring over a cut of meat. The *hoplomachus* feinted with his spear, then lunged at his opponent, who blocked him with his shield but staggered back at the impact. He also missed his footing and had to catch himself quickly. The two men started circling again, as the crowd egged them on with catcalls and cheers.

"The older man will win," Carolyn said, considering the pair with a professional eye. "He's pretending to be weaker."

"What did she say?" Pompey asked, remembering her prowess from the previous day.

"She said the *murmillo* will win," Felix translated.

"I believe her." Turning to Crassus, Pompey said he would bet a dozen *aurei* that the *murmillo* would triumph. The general smiled and accepted the wager, adding Pompey never learned his lesson and always backed the weaker party.

The young man was closing in again. He kept thrusting his spear at his opponent's face, causing him to duck from side to side. Pressing home his attack the *hoplomachus* lunged and grazed the man's forearm. The *murmillo* avoided further harm to himself by striking with his shield and shoving back his rival. He was standing more than thirty metres from Felix, but the blood on his arm was no less glaring than had it been on a snowbank. The crowd was ecstatic.

"How far will they go?" Carolyn asked.

"It's up to Pompey to decide."

"You've got to be kidding."

"I told you not to watch."

The crowd's cheers and the sight of blood stirred the young man's zeal. With a bull-like roar he charged the *murmillo* and a dozen times his spear groped for his flesh, missing its target by no more than a hair. The mob was urging him on. "Skewer him!" cried a matronly woman near Felix. "Stab him like a chicken!" And his spear *was* poised for a final blow when the *murmillo* lashed out with his leg and swept the young man's feet from under him. In the process the latter dropped his shield. He flailed wildly with his spear, but the contest was over. Knocking the heavy spear aside, the older man stabbed down and pierced his rival's thigh.

The crowd was standing and shouting itself hoarse. "Celadus! Celadus!" they screamed — the *murmillo*'s name. For his part, the *hoplomachus* had rolled over on his side and was facing Pompey with his thumb upraised.

"Ask your sister if I should spare him," Pompey told Felix.

"I beg your pardon?"

"She has won me twelve gold pieces. She will decide if this man lives."

With a pang of horror, Felix translated Pompey's words. Carolyn was shocked when she heard his proposition.

"You mean to say, this man could be murdered in public?"

"I'm afraid so. Only this crowd doesn't think of it as murder. Instead it has a religious meaning."

"There you have it! Religion again! Still, my choice is simple. I'll let the man live."

"You can't. I mean, you're not allowed to decide."

"What do you mean?"

"We have to think about the butterfly effect. If you let him live, when he would otherwise die, you might substantially alter the future."

The blood drained from Carolyn's face. She knew he was right and she could not intervene, but a man would possibly die as a result. With a look of pain and utter disgust, she covered her eyes and ears with her *palla*.

"She seems upset," Pompey commented. "She can't make up her mind?"

"Our traditions don't allow us to meddle in life and death affairs," Felix explained, concealing the catch in his voice. "It is part of our Druidic way."

"All right," Pompey said, in an agreeable tone: like any good Roman he respected other people's customs. "I'll decide myself."

He stood and surveyed the mob in the stands. They were watching him in silence now, some with their thumbs upraised, a sign they wished the man to live, but the majority with their thumbs downturned. With a pitying glance at the figure in the sand, Pompey motioned downwards with his thumb. Murmuring parting words to his opponent, and stroking him with something close to affection, the *murmillo* stabbed him in the neck and killed him instantly.

The crowd almost choked on its excitement. Felix had to struggle hard to keep himself from vomiting.

"Is he dead?" Carolyn asked from under her *palla*.

"Yes," Felix croaked. "You were wise not to watch."

"There's religion for you," she sneered.

"Yes. But it will be religion that brings an end to this barbarity."

By now two new gladiators were squaring off with each other, a *thraex* and a *retiarius*. Aware that Felix was new to this game, Pompey began explaining the techniques of the *retiarius*, and how it took colossal skill to make good use of his net. Halfway through his explanation, someone called his name. Glancing round, Felix spied Cicero approaching; he was dragging an older man in his wake. The fiery glint in his eye stirred Felix's discomfort.

"See whom I have found," Cicero spoke, when he and his companion were standing beside Pompey.

"This is indeed a pleasure," Pompey exclaimed, clasping the old man's arm with his hand.

"*Adulescens*," Cicero continued, addressing Felix this time "Surely you recognize our friend?"

"No, *domine*."

"You don't?" Pompey asked, "How's that possible?"

"And how about you, Sextus? Do you recognize this foreigner?"

"I have never laid eyes on him," the older man spoke, "Are you sure he claims …?"

"Yes," Cicero announced. "He claims to be your adopted son."

Felix felt his limbs stiffen to ice. There had always been a chance that his story would be seen through, but the odds had seemed incredibly remote. Now he was confronted by a group of angry noblemen who knew that they'd been lied to and were insisting that he explain himself. Indeed, the slave Flaccus had seized his arm and was forcing it backwards, to prevent him from escaping and to make him talk. Sensing a threat, Carolyn had bared her head.

"Tell me who you are," Pompey demanded. "Quickly and without subterfuge."

"I am Felix, son of Belenus. I am from Prytan. My father is a Druid."

"Where did you learn your Latin?"

"And how did you know my name?" Aceticus asked.

"I have read your book, *magister*."

"I am working on a book, but it is only half completed."

"Who are you?" Pompey repeated, as Flaccus slapped Felix on the side of his head.

"Perhaps he's a slave," Crassus suggested. "That would explain his hateful comments last night."

"And it would explain why he asked me to conduct him south, into the thick of Spartacus's lair. Are you spying for that gladiator scum?"

Flaccus was poised to strike Felix again. As he lifted his hand, Carolyn caught it, twisted it down and forced him to his knees. Crassus grabbed at her, but she pivoted and tossed him on his back. Pompey seized her wrist and tried to slap her, but she performed a backwards flip, freeing herself and knocking him sideways. A nearby group witnessed the scene and applauded her for this show of gymnastics.

"Let's go," she told Felix, tugging at his toga. She didn't notice Flaccus: he'd drawn a dagger and was bearing down on her. Felix intervened. As he pushed Carolyn sideways, the blade plunged into him.

It struck him in his left side, just below his ribs. He gasped. The pain was instantaneous and like nothing he had ever felt: it was as if he were being pummeled by an unending series of halo balls. He glanced down. He was bleeding profusely.

"I'm hit," he said, as the sky seemed to brighten and grow more remote.

"Bloody cutthroats!" he heard Carolyn swear. She kicked Flaccus in the stomach and knocked him flat on his face. Crassus was about to throw a punch, but she shoved him into Pompey, who was looming up on her right. Using his toga as a sling, she bundled Felix on her back.

"Hang on tight," she gasped. "We have to leave this building."

With that said, she hopped onto a nearby stranger. Even as he crumpled beneath their weight, she vaulted from him onto a second pair of shoulders, then to a third, a fourth, a line of others, with such speed and precision that no one could respond to her movements. From behind they heard Pompey ordering them to stop. Felix was clinging to Carolyn's back, and flinching every time she twisted: he was drenched with blood and trembling with cold.

She was running toward an arch at the back that would lead directly to the building's exit. Five guards were standing idly about. At the sight of her onrush, and the sound of Pompey's shouts to stop the pair, the legionnaires formed a line to block her. But they weren't fast enough. Feinting left, she knocked one soldier down, who crashed into his buddy and threw the rest of them off balance. A few seconds later they had escaped the building.

"What now?" Carolyn gasped. "Felix! Stay with me!"

"We're on the building's south side," he groaned. "Look in front of you. You should see a temple, not too far from us ...."

The fire in his side cut his breathing short. By now his toga was horribly stained and he could barely keep his eyes from closing. But he was alert enough to hear the angry cries behind them.

"There they are!" Pompey was yelling. "They're heading for Mercury's Temple! We'll trap them there!"

A furious chase ensued. Carolyn was starting to tire — Felix could hear her gasping for breath, even as she tightened her grip on the toga to compensate for his own slackening hold. His head lolled. Behind them he saw six men closing in. They were fifteen metres off, ten, eight, six.... One of them was smiling, like a predator about to sink his teeth into his prey.

And then they were climbing a flight of marble steps. They had reached the temple precinct. Almost sobbing with the effort, Carolyn cleared the steps and approached the *cella*'s door. It clattered as she shoved it open — and struck their lead pursuer in the nose. She leaped inside and slammed the door behind them. The dark encompassed them like a suit of armour.

A moment later their pursuers appeared. Although they did not dare to enter the *cella* — it was a space reserved for priests alone — they scoured the inner chamber for traces of their quarry. Confusion took the place of rage: apart from a trail of blood on the floor, there was no sign whatsoever of the mysterious siblings.

Chapter Ten

Although the process was uncomfortable, Felix was glad when the TPM engaged and hurled him into the distant future. One moment he could see his pursuers by the door; the next he was being stretched like putty toward a world in which these people had been dead two thousand years. For an instant, too, his pain subsided, only to resurface as his limbs snapped back to normal.

But wait. Was something off …?

He was on the floor and staring up at a ceiling. Instead of totalium, it was built of panelled stone. Beside him was the statue from Mercury's temple, but there were many other sculptures, too, from Greco-Roman times. The TPM team was nowhere to be seen; a crowd was milling about instead, dressed in the strangest clothes and conversing in a language that wasn't Common Speak.

"Felix? Can you hear me?" Carolyn spoke. She was standing nearby and panting still, "We're not in our time. I think your wound affected our trajectory...."

Her words were cut off by a piercing scream. By now a woman had spotted them; in particular, she had seen the blood-soaked toga. Her cries attracted other people's notice, and a horrified crowd took shape around the pair.

"What are they saying?" Carolyn asked.

"They're speaking English," Felix gasped. "And I recognize this space. It's a famous museum in New York City; it's called the Metropolitan."

He couldn't speak any more. His wound was bleeding, the world was spinning, and the light around him was growing dimmer.

"Hang on," Carolyn whispered. "Help is on the way."

Sure enough, a guard approached, followed by paramedics and three armed guards. They were speaking into clumsy looking gadgets, and one man was trying to wave her back. She grasped Felix's hand — to signal that she wouldn't be parted from her friend.

The crowd was eyeing her with suspicion — her Roman garments didn't help. She ignored them and stuck like glue to Felix, even when the paramedics wheeled him off on a gurney. When an armed man tried to hold her in place, she vaulted over him and made the spectators gasp. And as the paramedics steered the gurney down a hallway, past an exit to a vehicle that was backed up on a sidewalk, she was right beside it and clutching onto Felix. A man tried to block her from entering the ambulance, but she brushed him off and took a seat inside.

The vehicle moved off. Under different circumstances she might have enjoyed herself: she'd heard about cars but never dreamed she would ride in one. She'd never imagined either that she would see a city filled with such machines, all of them exhaling fumes into the air — an unthinkable act of rudeness in her era. At the same time, she observed the pedestrians' fashions: how quaint and out-of-date they were, consisting of fabrics like wool and cotton, instead of carbon-fibres and moulded plastics. Was this real or was it a simulation of a bygone age?

She glanced at Felix, who was attached to an IV. Carolyn had studied the history of medicine and recognized this old equipment. A mask was on his mouth and a monitor tracked his heart rate. Human beings, not drones, were supervising these procedures. She found this very odd and … worrying.

"You saved my life," she whispered. "Please don't die."

The ambulance came to a stop. Two men swiftly unloaded the stretcher and wheeled it past a sliding door into a hall that was full of uniformed people. It also contained outdated equipment, wheelchairs, defibrillators, ECG scans, and ungainly computers: Carolyn guessed this was a health facility.

Three people huddled around Felix and probed his wounds. Carolyn was wondering when they would place him in a life-pod, to stabilize his heart rate and metabolic levels. They could then inject him with recombinative tissue, let him sleep a few hours, and send him packing. Instead, they wheeled him into an operating theatre, cutting at his toga and tunic as they moved. When Carolyn tried to follow, a sturdy nurse blocked her path. Kind but insistent, she steered her to a seat in the nearby waiting room.

An hour passed with depressing slowness. Patients kept appearing in droves, some stooped over, some wailing in pain, and some dripping blood all over. Was the entire population sick, she wondered? To distract herself from this circus show, she glanced at a newspaper that was lying on the seat beside her. She studied it with interest. She had heard of newspapers, but never handled one before. Flipping through its pages, she found the use of so much paper wasteful. And it would take several hours to absorb this writing, as opposed to downloading it through a cortical implant.

Although the text escaped her, she did discover one fact. No sooner had it registered than two men in uniforms sidled near. They started asking questions, which she couldn't answer, not even when one of them spoke in a language he called *Español*. They wrote something down using paper and pencils — how primitive these people were — then motioned her to sit again and await their return.

As soon as they were gone, she hurried to the room where she'd seen Felix last — a good thing, too. The sturdy nurse was about to wheel him off. Catching sight of Carolyn, she waved her forward and the pair of them walked through a different pair of doors and down a long hallway until they paused outside an elevator.

"Felix," Carolyn spoke. "It's me. Wake up."

"Carolyn," he groaned, opening his eyes a crack, "I overheard the doctor say I'm bleeding inside and they can't stop it. They can't operate, either, because I've lost too much fluid. They'll try tomorrow, once I've had a transfusion, but it doesn't look good."

"What's the matter with these jerks? They don't know about recombinative tissue? We prepared it last year in my biology class!"

The door wheeled open and the nurse steered the gurney on board. A man and woman were chatting inside — they were wearing ID cards and were part of the staff. Entering the space, Carolyn bumped into the woman and nodded her apologies.

"Listen closely," Felix resumed. "You must complete our mission. That's the only thing that counts. The problem is the obvious temples won't work. Do you remember what the doctor said? If a temple's been exposed too long, the portal will have lost its 'charge'? That means —"

"Save your strength. You'll tell me later."

"I have to tell you now!"

"I'm not leaving without you, that's all there is to it. By the way," she added, to change the subject, "I know today's date — I saw it in a newspaper. It's September 10, 2001. So we're two hundred years away from our era...."

"Did you say September 10, 2001?" If her intention had been to calm him, she had miserably failed. If anything, his face was even paler now.

"Yes. Why?"

"That means tomorrow is 9/11. The twin towers are about to be attacked." He said "twin towers" in English, and the nurse overheard him.

"The twin towers?" she joked. "Are you planning a tour?"

The elevator stopped. With Carolyn's help, she wheeled Felix out and along a hallway to unit 501. She then told Carolyn, using Felix to translate, that there was a sitting room at the end of the hallway where she should wait until she was summoned to see him. There were tests to be run and she would get in people's way.

"I'll be back soon," she said. "Promise me you'll last."

"Listen," Felix said, "the famous temples won't work...."

"Tell me later. And I'm serious. You can't die in my absence."

She stooped and, to his surprise, pecked him on the forehead. She then turned on her heel and moved toward the waiting room before Felix could utter another word of protest. The nurse smiled and wheeled him alongside a bed. Together with another nurse whom she called in from the floor's front desk, she transferred him to a mattress, gave him an injection, plumped his pillow, and covered him with blankets. Explaining they had other patients to look after, she left the unit.

Felix stared out the window. The sun had set and the world outside was filled with shadows. Central Park lay sprawled before him and, beyond it, a line of buildings that were sporadically lit. In the sky above he spied the planet Jupiter. He thought about his mother and how she would grace its moon in two hundred years.

The medication was kicking in — the throbbing in his side had stopped. Maybe he could sleep; he was tired enough. But the day's date kept gnawing at him — it was as pointed as the blade with which Flaccus had stabbed him. September 10, 2001. He had seen the footage of the planes striking home, and knew that events for the next fifty years could be traced to that particular crisis. It was because of 9/11 that the "religious wars" had broken out, ones that had pushed the world to the brink of extinction. That was when a world government had started, why religions of all types had been collectively abandoned, why one language (Common Speak) had come to prevail, and why people were encouraged to curtail their emotions, hence the start of the ERR program. The past had been downplayed, too, because it was believed its grievances would stir people's passions and cause the cycle of violence to continue.

By now Felix was delirious. The room was spinning and, in the encompassing shadow, he forgot where he was, when he was … who he was. Visions hit home of exploding buildings, dead gladiators, his father's corpse, and crowds of people, billions of souls, breaking out in red spots and breathing their last. At one point he saw Flaccus again, flinched as light glittered off his blade, and could feel cold steel slipping into his gut.

"Stop!" he yelled, striking out.

Part of him was horrorstruck. This wasn't any dream. Someone was above him and restraining his arms. Death. And a shank of metal was sticking in his flank, past his skin and muscle, past his pancreas and kidney, to release a witch's brew that burned each cell in its path. Death. He tried to speak, but the pain cut him off. Death. He

punched again then darkness absorbed him, like a rogue
wave sweeping over a ship and dragging its passengers
and crew to sea bottom.

"Death," he whispered, with the last of his breath.

There was nothing. The world had stopped revolving;
light and time itself had ceased. He was nowhere and
everywhere, and past and future were rolled together.

Except ... Was it his imagination or was someone
calling?

"Felix, Felix, Felix," it repeated.

"Leave me alone," he muttered. "I'm supposed to
be dead."

"Wake up, Felix," the voice insisted. It sounded a lot
like Carolyn. Something slapped his cheek, not just once
but several times. His eyes fluttered open and, yes, she
was looming above him. Instead of her *palla*, she was
dressed in jeans and an old sweatshirt. She was also carrying a primitive laptop. And light was flooding into the
room: the sky was blue and achingly pretty.

"It's about time you awoke."

"What's going on? How ...?"

Smiling thinly, she recounted how she'd fixed everything. Her priority had been to visit the lab. Waiting
until the staff had left for the evening, she had entered

it using a card she had "lifted" — from that woman she'd collided with the day before. Despite the lab's outdated equipment, she had "brewed" a measure of recombinative tissue. In the dark of night she'd entered his unit and injected him with this restorative mix. To judge by his complexion, it had taken effect.

"I do feel better," Felix admitted. "My wound isn't nearly as sore."

"Just take it easy," Carolyn warned. "You'll spend another day here and we'll discuss our next step."

She was about to leave and get them breakfast, when the nurse from the previous day entered the room. In contrast to her pleasant expression, she was frowning now and bristling with suspicions. In fact, she was blocking the door with her frame.

"Why did you mention them yesterday?" she spat.

"Mention what?" Felix asked.

"The twin towers. They've been attacked. And you knew that they would be — I could see it on your face. You're a terrorist, aren't you? An inside man or something."

"This is ridiculous," Felix said, half rising from the bed. The nurse took this as a threatening sign and backed toward the door.

"Stay where you are. I'm calling in security."

But even as she spoke, the PA system announced her name. It directed her to proceed to ER 6 as a wave of casualties was streaming in. With a hard expression, she stepped toward the door. Before exiting, she spun and hissed at the pair, "This isn't over!" That said, she left and locked the door behind her.

"We have to leave," Carolyn said matter-of-factly. Without another word, she opened a window and ducked outside. As Felix struggled to his feet, she returned moments later through the unit's door with pants, a sweater, and runners in hand: the sweater still had a hanger stuck inside it. Understanding she had scaled the wall and entered the building through a nearby window, Felix grinned and slipped into the pants.

"Put the rest on later. We have to leave."

She ushered him from the room and down a hallway. His wound was raw and he couldn't move quickly, but he didn't want her carrying him again. As it turned out, they'd vacated the room just in time. Two guards were already closing in on the unit.

"This way," Carolyn said, entering a stairwell. With some help from her, he could navigate the stairs. His wound felt as if a dog were biting him, but he was glad to be up and moving about. Maybe death wasn't ready to claim him yet.

They reached the ground floor and emerged from the stairwell. Felix was wearing the sweater and runners and was still clutching onto the hanger — he was thinking it might come in handy later. They rounded another corner and Carolyn pinched him: thirty metres in front of them was the hospital's main exit. Personnel were rushing back and forth as ambulances and taxicabs dropped dust-stained, coughing people off.

"It's perfect," Carolyn murmured. "They won't notice us leave."

Straightening their clothes, they drew near the exit, sidestepping nurses, orderlies, and doctors who were frantically trying to deal with the wounded. Halfway to their destination, a light above the exit flashed and an alarm sounded shrilly. The guard lifted a phone, listened intently, then jumped to his feet and started scanning the crowd. Seconds later, his eyes took them in. He spoke into the phone and strolled aggressively toward them.

"Keep walking," Carolyn said, handing him the laptop she was carrying. "Don't break your stride and don't look back."

He followed her instructions. There was the sound of a body being tossed to the floor and he understood she had "handled" the guard. A moment later there were two more thuds — friends of the guard had been similarly dispatched. Resisting the temptation to glance behind, he pushed a door open and passed outside.

The air was delicious. The temperature was perfect and the sky was beautiful — the segment of sky to the

north of them at least. Down south it was a different story.
Huge plumes of greenish grey hung over the city, like
vampires intent on sucking blood from their victims. The
streets, too, were packed with traffic, none of it south-
bound except for fire trucks and police cars. Pedestrians
overcrowded the sidewalks, as an enormous chain of men
and women were intent on escaping the chaos downtown.
They were silent for the most part, dust-covered and confused. Sirens were reverberating faintly in the distance and
seemed to tear the very air in two. As Felix examined the
crowd in fascination, Carolyn approached.

"Ten more guards are coming," she warned him.

Wordlessly, he started walking, the laptop and wire
hanger in hand. At the end of the block, he turned the
corner and looked around. There. Ten metres ahead of
him lay the entrance to a parking lot. With Carolyn urging him to hurry up, he led her past an empty booth —
the guard was probably watching events unfold — and
headed down a spiral driveway. Sprawled before them
was a selection of cars. Felix eyed them carefully, search-
ing for one with a nondescript exterior. He found what
he was after: a dark grey compact with shaded windows.

"It's locked," Carolyn said, trying the door. "What
now?"

"You'll see." Felix handed her the laptop and straightened the hanger. He then manoeuvred its hook past the

window's weatherstripping and snaked it into the door's interior. Fishing around carefully, he latched onto the locking bar and drew it back with a loud, metallic click. The door opened smoothly.

"Climb in. Quick."

"But what about the engine?"

"Don't worry about that. Check the glove compartment — that little box in front of you — and see if there are any tools inside."

Wrestling with the steering wheel, he ripped its access cover off. He then groped about carefully until he found two wires whose insulation he scratched, thereby exposing the underlying metal. Twisting these together, his fingers teased another wire out which he brushed against the other two. There was a sputtering sound and he pressed down on the gas. The engine came to life.

"Amazing," Carolyn cried. "And I found some scissors. Will they help?"

Felix pressed the scissors' blades into a crack between the wheel and steering column. Applying force to their handles, he disengaged a pin. Formerly locked, the wheel turned easily. Carolyn was impressed.

"Where did you learn these tricks?" she asked, "It wasn't from reading Virgil, I'll bet."

"I spent lots of time in the car museum," he grunted. "The curator liked me and taught me things — how to drive cars, how to fix them, how to steal one in a pinch. I never thought I'd be able to put his lessons to use."

"We're just in time," Carolyn said, pointing to their right. Sure enough, several guards had appeared and were scouring the space for signs of the pair. As Felix eased the compact forward, one guard glanced in their direction. Unable to see past the shaded glass, he shrugged his shoulders and let them pass. Carefully, Felix drove toward the exit, expecting to hear shouts or maybe even gunshots. There was nothing.

Moments later they joined the northbound traffic and were just one of thousands of cars on the road.

Chapter Eleven

Felix climbed outside the car and surveyed his surroundings. After navigating Manhattan for at least three hours, they had finally left the island via the George Washington Bridge. They had headed along the New Jersey Turnpike until the needle on the gas gauge had dipped close to empty and they'd been forced to exit near a large shopping complex. An enormous building stood some fifty metres off, full of stores and restaurants and movie theatres, yet the place was dead. People had gone home because of the attacks in New York City. With her retinal upgrades, Carolyn could see smoke in the east, ghostly remnants from the obliterated towers.

"This is it," Felix asked. "Do you think it will work?"

"Let's find out and see," Carolyn replied, opening her laptop on the hood of the car. "This computer's pretty primitive, but I rearranged the chips inside. It should serve our purpose, in other words. And this area's wired. We have Internet access."

"Great. Let's search for a bank online."

"Any bank will do. I still can't believe the encryption is so primitive."

Punching words into a search engine, Felix found what they were after and let Carolyn take over. Despite her clumsiness in working the keypad — she was used to cortical implants and "thinking" her commands — she "stormed" the bank's firewall and entered its mainframe. Toying with the program, she created an account containing a million dollars. Typing in additional commands, she enabled them to withdrawal cash from any ATM at large, merely by punching in a sequence of numbers.

"Let's go," she said, closing her laptop.

Minutes later they were in the mall and standing at an automated teller. She entered the code she had arranged on the mainframe and a flashing prompt asked how much money she wanted. She punched in $800 — the maximum limit. Seconds later she was counting a stack of twenty dollar bills.

"We've just helped ourselves to someone's money," Felix said. "Won't this trigger a butterfly effect?"

"The million dollars I deposited comes from millions of separate accounts. No one will feel a few missing cents any more than the owner of that stolen car will be affected once the cops have tracked his property down."

"We're breaking a lot of laws here."

"Who's to know? And we have no choice if we're going to save our future."

"I suppose that makes sense."

"Come on," she said, yanking him forward. "Lunch is on me."

"Are you finishing ... what are they called again?"

"French fries," Felix answered. "Help yourself. And you should try this sugar beverage. My 3L Domestic System would never let me drink this stuff."

They were in a diner a mile away from the ATM they'd "patronized." In front of them were the remnants of a meal that Felix had only seen in old-fashioned movies: hamburgers, nachos, Tex-Mex, and French fries. As different as the food was from the nutrition they were used to, the detail that impressed them most was the kitchen at the back of the diner. They couldn't believe humans would cook their own food.

"Would you like another Coke?" the waitress asked, with a friendly smile.

"I'm fine, thank you."

"Where are you two coming from?"

"New York City."

"Oh my goodness. You were lucky to escape the destruction. I wonder what those terrorists were thinking, to kill so many folks like that."

On the verge of tears, the waitress retreated. Felix translated what she'd said, leading Carolyn to mutter something about unstable emotions. Smiling at her intolerance, Felix changed the topic.

"I've been thinking about our next step."

"Oh?"

"There's no point travelling to famous temples like the Parthenon. They've been exposed to the elements for hundreds of years and their "charge" vanished centuries ago."

"You're right," Carolyn mused, staring down at her plate. "That means we're stuck here, doesn't it?"

"Not quite. There's one portal that might be operable still. Doctor Lee charged dozens of temples, including the one my dad discovered."

"So?"

"It was buried in an earthquake in 160 BC — three generations before Pompey's era. When my dad excavated it — or will excavate it two hundred years from now — no human had entered it in over two thousand years. So I'm thinking its charge is still intact. But it lies in France, in a town called Nimes...."

Carolyn placed her laptop on the table.

"What would we need?" she asked, "to travel to France?"

Felix thought for a moment. "Well," he said, "in addition to money, we'll need tickets and passports. Air travel from the U.S. will be restricted for days — or so I recall — and we'll have to fly from Canada if we're going to leave tomorrow."

"It's amazing how they still have separate countries," Carolyn said, motioning Felix to surf the web. He found the website for the U.S. State Department, the agency responsible for American passports, then handed the machine back to Carolyn. Hacking into the mainframe, she created two files with their personal data, noted that their documents had been approved, then searched a database of photographs.

"Here's one," she said, pausing on a picture of a boy who looked like Felix.

"There's some resemblance but ..."

"We're not finished yet."

Extracting this picture, together with one of a girl, she accessed an online photo lab. Using its software, she altered the two pictures until their subjects bore a sharp resemblance to themselves. She then uploaded them to their passport files on the State Department site. Finally, each passport was marked as an emergency order, with delivery no later than midnight that evening.

"What address should they deliver them to?" she asked.

"Let's see," he mused, surfing the net. "There's a hotel called the Sheraton near Buffalo, New York. If we're crossing into Canada we'll pass that way. You may as well give it as our delivery address."

With this taken care of, she created a credit card account, linking it to the bank account that she'd created by 'borrowing' pennies from several million people. It was then an easy matter to book two flights from Toronto to Nimes, with a brief stopover in Paris, France. Altogether these transactions had taken fifteen minutes.

"Would you care for dessert?" the waitress asked, returning with two menus.

"What do you have?"

"We have pies and brownies, but I recommend the chocolate cheesecake."

"We'll try the cheesecake," Felix said with a laugh. "With ice cream on the side."

"I'm thirsty," Felix announced. "*S'il vous plait,*" he called to the stewardess. "*Un autre jus d'orange si ça ne vous dérange pas.*"

They were flying in a passenger plane, and were half an hour from the city of Nimes. So far, everything had gone without hitch: their passports had been waiting at the Sheraton in Buffalo; they had crossed into Canada without awakening suspicions; they had driven to Pearson Airport, near Toronto, where their tickets had been waiting at the Air France gate; and their flight to Paris had been exactly on time, as had their connecting flight to Nimes.

"You really are something," Carolyn commented.

"Why? Because I'm thirsty?"

"How many languages do you speak?"

"I don't know. A lot of them, I guess. My dad always said that language is like food: each one has a different 'taste' and lends your 'diet' a certain spice."

"It's a talent," she mused. "I thought your skills were useless before, but I've been proven wrong." Embarrassed that she'd praised him, she changed the subject. "Will you look at that?" She was frowning now, "That woman keeps kissing the cross around her neck."

"It's a symbol of her faith. She's scared of flying and hopes —"

"That God will keep her safe?"

"Something like that."

"God didn't save those people in the towers, did He?"

"In actual fact, they were killed in God's name — a different god, at least."

"It's so irrational and disgusting …"

"But the firemen and cops who came to their rescue, and died in their attempt to save their fellow man, did so in God's name, some of them at least."

"That's irrational, too."

"Big deal, so humans are irrational."

Carolyn was about to retort, then changed her mind and looked outside. It wasn't rational to reason with an irrational person.

"*Bienvenue en France,*" the border guard spoke, holding out his hand for Felix's passport.

"*Voila monsieur,*" Felix replied. "*Il fait beau dehors.*"

Their plane had landed in Nimes and they were standing in the airport's terminal. Now that they were nearing their goal, both were anxious to reach the hidden temple.

"Ah, you are American," the official continued. "And these passports are brand new." He glanced down at some papers on his desk and suppressed the slightest frown.

"Yes," Felix replied in French. "We got them recently, just in time for our trip."

"The French people are sorry for the attacks on your country."

"Thank you. It was a black day for all civilized people."

"How long will you be staying in France, Monsieur Taylor?"

"A week."

"I see. One moment please."

The official left his booth, with their passports in hand. Felix looked at Carolyn, who, despite her calm expression, was suddenly full of suspicion.

"He suspects us," she said. "He glanced at something on his desk."

"Maybe it was a newspaper." He stood on his tiptoes and glanced inside the booth. A gasp escaped him.

There was a picture of him and Carolyn. In it she was holding a stack of twenty-dollar bills. With a stab of fear he realized the photo had been snapped at the ATM in that large shopping complex. And there were two more pictures: one showed Carolyn "handling" a guard; the other a shot of them in the Pearson airport.

"They're onto us," Felix murmured.

"I can see that," Carolyn said, surveying the room. "There are plainclothes guards surrounding us. We'll have to fight our way out."

"Wait," Felix cautioned. "The guard's returning."

"I'm sorry for the delay," he apologized, resuming his seat. "Everything is fine. Enjoy your stay in France."

"We can go?"

"Of course."

"Excellent. *Merci bien monsieur*."

"*Je vous en prie*."

They walked toward the exit, expecting a horde of policemen to attack. Much to their surprise, they were left alone. They changed their American money into Euros, consulted a detailed map of the region, purchased tickets, and boarded a bus, one that would take them into downtown Nimes — all without any police interference.

"Why are they waiting?" Carolyn asked, taking a seat.

"I think I know," Felix said. "The American authorities must have tracked our movements. They suspect we're terrorists and notified the French police."

"But that still doesn't explain ..."

"They're following us and hoping that we'll take them to our leaders."

"I see," Carolyn said, glancing cautiously outside. "There are two cars behind us and another in front. What do we do?"

Felix frowned. They couldn't be arrested. With those photos as evidence, the cops could charge them with all sorts of crimes, and that meant they might spend a lot of time in prison. They had no choice: they had to elude these agents.

"The entrance to the temple lies inside a church. What street are we on?"

"It's called … General Leclerc."

"All right, we're getting close."

"Are you sure?"

"I've seen my father's temple at least fifty times. The city looks different from the version I know, but its basic layout is pretty much the same. In other words, I'm sure."

For the next few minutes Carolyn observed their pursuers, being careful not to appear too obvious. One car was beside them and she spied its passenger: he was lean, clean-shaven, and had a device in his ear. He was also cradling a vicious-looking pistol.

"We're leaving Feucheres Boulevard," Felix said. "Prague Boulevard should be coming up. There, I see the church. It's over on our right."

A minute later they exited the bus which had stopped fifty metres from the church's entrance. After passing a line of magnificent plane trees, they advanced on the church with its majestic tower and oaken doors. Not that there was time to take this grandeur in. The cars had stopped behind them and they had agents on their tail.

Mounting a flight of steps, they entered the building. The dim lighting inside took some getting used to and, without breaking his stride, Felix hurried to a candle display. Helping himself to a taper and some matches, he led Carolyn down a limestone aisle to the apse at the back, passing a series of somber Gothic arches. As they ran, she grabbed a pair of prayer books. Behind him he heard the church's door bang open.

They'd reached the apse. Once there, he opened a small wooden door and descended a spiral staircase to the church's crypt. Detaching herself, Carolyn crouched and fiddled with the door. She then joined Felix, taking three steps at a time.

"I wedged the books into the door frame. That should buy us some time."

"Those are prayer books, you realize."

"Then this is the best use they've ever been put to."

They proceeded to a brick wall at the back of this space. The only light came from a thirty-watt bulb, but Felix could discern a cross that had been carved into the wall in medieval times. He groped about.

"They're banging on the door," Carolyn informed him.

"There's a passageway behind this wall that was used in times of war. It leads to the building's ancient foundations and these include my father's temple. Now if I can just find the locking mechanism...."

"You might want to hurry," she said. "They've opened the door."

Sure enough, there was a bang above and the sound of clattering footsteps.

"There!" he cried in triumph, as a stretch of wall pivoted some ninety degrees. "Let's go!"

They just had time to slip behind the wall and shove it into place when the agents rushed in. Their voices were muffled but they were clearly bewildered.

"Hang on," Felix whispered, fumbling with his matches. "There, that's better."

The dark retreated as the match burst into life. As he'd expected from his previous visits, they were in a narrow passageway that stretched off to their right. The place was thick with dust and cobwebs, and beetles recoiled at the touch of the light. Shivering and feeling a touch claustrophobic, he moved forward with Carolyn mere inches behind.

"Be careful," he warned. "There's a hole on our left ..."

Carolyn squeaked and almost vanished from sight; she had been leaning to her left and fallen through a gap in the wall. If Felix hadn't grabbed her, she would have tumbled to her death. Unfortunately, he dropped his candle and it fell into the abyss. The dark swooped around them as if devouring them whole.

"Thanks," Carolyn gasped. "That was close."

"At least you found the entrance. Let me light another match...."

"That's not necessary." Opening her laptop, she powered it up. Its screen cast a ghostly glow and kept the shadows at bay. They peered into the hole beside them: it was about a metre wide and lined with stone and had possibly served as a well in times past. Securing her laptop to her waist with her belt, Carolyn ducked into this "well" and thrust her hands against its sides.

"Come on," she said. "It's not that bad."

Felix followed suit. Copying Carolyn's movements, he wormed his way down. At one point he almost lost his grip when a particularly large insect explored his back; but a minute later they had reached the bottom.

"The battery's weakening," Carolyn said. Sure enough, the laptop's glow was fading.

"That's okay. We're there," Felix answered, pointing to a slab of wood which he shoved to one side. "This was the temple's main entrance. Beyond it —"

"Just go," Carolyn said. "While we still have some light."

Beyond the wood was yet another space, half-filled with dirt and rotting timber. In the thick of this debris he spied the outline of a statue — an arm upraised in a gesture of greeting. He knew this was Diana, virgin goddess of the hunt.

"That's it," he exclaimed. "If we walk forward one metre, the TPM should kick in."

"So what are we waiting for?"

"Hand me your laptop. You can't take it across the portal."

With a growl of impatience, she closed its lid and passed the computer to him. Retreating several steps, feeling his way in the dark, Felix shoved the laptop into a massive hollow that was deep enough to hide it from his father's pick and shovel — two hundred years into the future. With this task accomplished, he rejoined Carolyn and they stumbled to the statue of the goddess. Without warning an orb of blinding light engulfed them.

Having received its first visitors in over two thousand years, the sacred space was empty again.

Chapter Twelve

The temporal projection was different this time. Felix's limbs were impossibly stretched and a tunnel of light was glowing around him, but now, instead of one opening before him, there were "holes" all over through which events could be seen, fleetingly, like images in a high speed film. There were riders on horses, farmers seeding fields, a battle scene of epic proportions, and a building easily the size of a city. A cacophony of sound exploded, of laughter, terror, excitement, and rage, as well as the strains of impossibly sweet music....

"Felix ...!"

He flinched. That was Carolyn calling. Spinning in slow motion, he could see that she had slipped into a gap and that her stretched-out features were snapping back to normal. Had she fallen out of the temporal vortex?

With a supreme act of will, he reversed his course midway through the tunnel — his elongated limbs were bending back on themselves, so that now they extended in both directions. He focused on the spot where Carolyn had vanished and.... There!

She was lying in a desolate landscape. It consisted of a grey sky and a lake of mud, with clumps of grass breaking through the ooze. Where was she? Or rather ... when was she?

The mud's surface parted and an appendage emerged — it was over two metres long and tipped with a needle. A second one rose up, a third, a dozen, until these objects numbered in the hundreds. They were converging on Carolyn, who was up to her knees in the slop.

Claws broke forth, two to each appendage. They were accompanied by tube-like structures that contained multiple eyes, jet black and unblinking. Felix's blood practically froze. What ...?

Scorpions! They were scorpions! But they were fantastically huge! Somehow Carolyn had entered an era when monstrosities like these had walked the earth!

She didn't scream — her ERR prevented that — but the look on her face was one of desperation. With no weapon in hand, she'd bunched her fists together and was girding herself for a pointless show of combat.

Concentrating hard, Felix extended an arm. Although the sensation was excruciating — it felt as if he were sticking his hand in boiling tar — he saw his arm materialize in that prehistoric world. Stretching farther, he managed to tap Carolyn's shoulder. She flinched, thinking she was under attack, then grabbed his hand and jumped in his direction, even as he hauled at her with all his strength. She felt a stinger brush her hair, missing her by inches....

And then she was in the vortex and her proportions were distorted. A shower of light beams was propelling them forward, toward a space of dust and shadow. An eternity later (although it was only an instant) they were thrown into this unknown setting, even as their limbs assumed their normal shape.

"Are you okay?" Felix asked, climbing to his feet.

"Thanks to you," she panted. "But ... where are we?"

Reassured that she was safe, he examined their setting. Light was entering through a far-off window and revealed that they were surrounded by ... books. The room's entire width, which measured fifty metres, was full of cases that stood a metre from each other, allowing enough space for someone to pass. Each case rose from the floor to the ceiling and continued for the length of the room — far into the shadows away from the windows. The shelves themselves were packed with books of every shape, size, and colour. The air was thick with disintegrating paper, a rich smell that made Felix think of ... his father.

He knew exactly where he was.

"We're back," he informed Carolyn. "We're in the Book Repository. The statue from the temple attracted us here."

He pointed to a statue of Diana in an alcove. The goddess's arm was raised in greeting — a sight he had seen on countless occasions.

"Thank goodness," Carolyn sighed. "We actually made it." She stopped a moment and considered Felix. He had approached his father's old-fashioned desk and was running his finger along its green-baize surface.

"We should tell my father we've arrived," she said gently.

He nodded and motioned to a black cube on the desk. She looked at it and almost managed a smile.

"I thought Speakboxes vanished decades ago."

"My father's old-fashioned. That Speakbox is the only piece of technology in here."

"It's more than adequate. General Manes," she spoke, addressing the cube.

"Processing," the cube replied. A moment later it was playing a message.

"This is General Isaiah Manes. Please leave me a voiceprint."

"That's odd," Carolyn mused. "He never fails to answer when I call. Is there a Holo-port nearby?"

"There's one across the street, in the Nano-Center. It's over this way."

Leading Carolyn through a warren of shelves, he hurried to the exit in the building's northeast corner. There were window wells along the wall, although most had been filled in over the past few decades. And the ceiling, although worn, was highly ornate, an indication that the space had been a place of elegance.

"Where are we?" she asked.

"This building was something called a department store. It was called Hudson's Bay and was at one time very popular. It should have been razed, but the Federation preserved it for historical reasons. It seemed the perfect choice for a book repository."

By now they'd left the building through a pair of glass doors and were crossing Road 11 (formerly Yonge Street), a four-tiered thoroughfare that was the city's central artery. Felix looked around. The area was the same: its totalium towers dwarfed his father's building; the streets and sidewalks were immaculately swept; every pane of glass had been brought to a shine; and there was an ion crackle splitting the air, a sign the Weather

Template was planning rain for that evening. On the other hand, there wasn't a soul in the streets, no shoppers, no businessmen, no tourists, no one. The lack of any human presence made the district feel … unsettling.

"There's the Nano-Center," Felix cried, suppressing a shiver.

They hastened into a nearby tower that, with its exceptional height and swivelling dome, was the city's crowning landmark. It too betrayed no signs of life except for a screen by the entrance to a Vacu-lift. Ignoring it, they approached a Holo-port at the far end of the lobby. Reciting her log-in code and her dad's contact number, she waited for the link to engage. Sure enough, an image of her father took shape.

"This is General Isaiah Manes," the hologram spoke. "Please leave me a voiceprint." The image popped, like a bubble bursting.

"I don't understand …" Carolyn started to say.

"Contact Doctor Lee," Felix said. "He'll tell us where your father is."

Again she recited her login code and the doctor's information. It took ten seconds for the link to register, and when the doctor's face came into focus, Carolyn and Felix felt their spines turn to water.

The hologram showed Doctor Lee slumped over in the cubicle where he'd discussed their mission with them. His hair was dishevelled, his chin unshaven, and his suit wrinkled and unfastened at its top. His black-ringed eyes met the Holo-port's lens and he projected an air of abject surrender.

"It is over," he murmured. "We have utterly failed. I offer my apologies to General Manes, to my colleagues, and every citizen at large. Although the gesture is a futile one, I feel I must do something to restore my honour. Please forgive me."

He brought a vial to his lips and swallowed deeply. There was a skull and crossbones on the vial's label and, an instant later, the doctor was dead. The Holo-port went blank and a calm voice offered to replay the message.

Felix was sweating. Despite her ERR, Carolyn looked nervous.

"I don't understand …" she said.

"I think I do," Felix replied, pointing to the Holo-port's console. "Look at today's date. It's October 15, 2214. For some strange reason, we've been gone a year."

"So …?"

"So we didn't find the *lupus ridens*. And scientists found no cure for the plague. That means the planet has been emptied of all human life."

Without awaiting her reaction, he strolled over to the lobby's Teledata screen. It featured World President Sajit Gupta. The speech was a recording — its upload

date was March 11 and that meant it had been playing for months on end. Felix stared at the broadcast.
Whereas the president was normally self-possessed, he
had lost his confidence and seemed badly rattled.

And his face was covered with scarlet spots.

"Dear citizens," he spoke, in a wavering voice.
"Please grant me your attention for a final broadcast
from your leader. It is with profound regret that I
announce we have been defeated by this plague.
Despite our best efforts, the virus has struck every
human on the planet, even those who strictly abided
by the curfew. Half our brothers and sisters have per-
ished, and the remainder are in orbit, waiting for the
inevitable to happen."

He paused, to regain his composure. To Felix's
amazement, he brushed a renegade tear from his eye.

"For millennia," he resumed, "we humans defeated
every threat to our survival, from predators and famine,
to political strife and global warming. At times we created
terrible havoc, delighting in war, savagery, and ignorance.
But as often as we proved destructive, we manifested
virtues that more than made up for our violence: inven-
tiveness, generosity, compassion, and open-mindedness.
Surely other intelligent beings, if they exist and one day
visit our planet, will have ample reason to condemn us for
our faults; but at the same time, studying our record as a

whole, they will gasp at our achievements and mourn the extinction of our grandeur."

He coughed and passed a hand across his brow: his strength was ebbing fast.

"Finally, you have noticed that I am speaking with emotion. This is because I have had my ERR reversed and am subject to a diversity of feelings. I have acted thus because I am convinced it is incumbent on me, as the last elected spokesman for our planet, to address you and my future non-human audience as a true and proud product of my species, with all my mental proclivities on display. We have come so far," he lamented, raising his eyes, "and with our demise, something rare and precious disappears — as light inevitably must dissolve into shadow." He lowered his eyes and faced the camera.

"God bless us all," he whispered. Then the screen went blank.

The recording ended, only to start again. His speech was too tragic to hear a second time, and Felix and Carolyn retreated from the screen. Standing by the building's exit, they were struggling to digest the unbearable truth: they were the only humans alive on the planet.

"Our plan is obvious," she finally spoke. "We'll grab a shuttle, board the space station, return to the past, and find the *lupus ridens*."

"We'd better get started," Felix agreed. "Before we're infected with the plague."

They passed outside and approached a Dispersion Portal: it would take them to the Shuttle Depot where they would pilot a craft and ride it to the TPM. They hadn't taken a dozen steps, however, when three Enforcement Drones swooped in. Blocking their path, the drones ordered them to stop.

"You are in violation of Presidential Order 3214T566 that specifies all civilians, unless formally exempted, shall remain under strict quarantine. Failure to comply with this directive involves immediate detention of no less than thirty days."

"Don't interfere," Carolyn protested. "We're on important business."

"You are in violation of Presidential Order 3214T566 …" the lead E.D. repeated, even as it closed in on the pair. A compartment opened and Felix watched as a stun-rod appeared: it could deliver 20,000 volts of electricity.

"They mean business," he whispered. "We'd better return to the Nano-Center."

"Remain where you are," the drone insisted, as they took to their heels. It followed in pursuit and would have zapped them for sure if Carolyn hadn't performed a backwards flip, landed on its CPU and crushed it flat. Before the other drones reacted, she joined Felix and they hurried into the Center. To keep the E.D.s from pouring in, she kicked a locking panel and smashed its circuitry to pieces.

"That should hold them," she said, as the drones let loose a siren and summoned reinforcements. "How do you propose we get to the depot?"

Felix stood there thinking. They couldn't be arrested. Being machines, the drones would carry out their orders and lock them away and therefore expose them to the plague. They had to reach the depot, but the question was how? In keeping with municipal code, there were no Portals inside the Nano-Center, and proceeding outside was out of the question, even if they took a different exit, as by now the drones would have the building surrounded. And they couldn't tunnel underground....

Or could they?

"Follow me!" Felix cried, heading to a door, which led to a staircase. Just as he suspected, there were stairs going down as well as up. Descending them two steps at a time, the pair reached the basement and the entrance to a storage space. This is where piles of scrap lay waiting: exercise chairs, executive think-pods, memory tanks, data-tubes, janitorial probes, and other ancient devices, all of them slated at some point for recycling. Looking past this junk that just years before had been state of the art, Felix searched for a distinctive marker.

"Why are we here?" Carolyn asked.

"Ages ago there were these underground tunnels. They had these metal tracks that cars would run on and carry people to different points in the city. One line ran the length of Road 11, with stations at this intersection and where the depot now stands."

"That's just an urban legend."

"No, they really existed. And the authorities never filled them in because they thought they might be needed in a crisis. The entrance would be marked with an 'S.'"

"There's an 'S' over there," she announced, motioning to her left.

"That's it!" he yelled. "What did I tell you?"

In a distant corner of that overcrowded space, beyond a stack of cortical implants, was a large "S" painted in fluorescent yellow. It was covered in dust and badly worn, but was visible still. Below it was a metal door.

Of course, it was locked. Felix was going to force it open, but Carolyn motioned to a box beside it. Blowing off a layer of dust, she uncovered a label on its plastic cover: "Break in the event of an emergency."

"This is an emergency," she mused, rapping the plastic with her knuckles. A moment later she extracted a key, which she inserted into a lock on the door. She manoeuvred it gingerly — the lock's pins were rusted — but a click rang out and the lock gave way.

They opened the door and stepped onto a stairwell that was set inside a vertical concrete shell. Glancing down, they guessed it was thirty metres high and, at its bottom, passed into the roof of a tunnel — the subway tunnel, or so Felix assumed. Before he could get a good look at the structure, he heard the E.D.'s vibrating in the distance. He closed the door — and cut their lighting off.

They descended the stairs, their footsteps echoing up and down its concrete hollows. The structure was old, slippery in places and, most alarming, jiggled at every step. They were glad when they reached its bottom without the metal collapsing.

"What now?" Carolyn asked. "It's pitch black in here...."

Even as she spoke a fluorescent light came alive – it had been activated by their movements, no doubt. It triggered a series of other lights, ones that stretched off in both directions and illuminated the tunnel and its rusted tracks. They also disclosed a band of shadows that vanished swiftly into the tunnel's cracks, indignant that their privacy was under assault.

"Are those rats?" Carolyn asked.

"I think they are. I guess the Vermin Sentries don't patrol this far. Come on."

Felix set off down the tunnel, following an arrow that pointed to "Union Station." The going wasn't easy.

There was a walkway to one side, but it was crumbled in places and required them to stick to the tracks. The problem here was that the wooden ties had rotted and provided them with little purchase for their feet. At the same time water was leaking in — there was the sound of dripping all about them — and some of it had gathered in substantial puddles. Thank goodness the third rail had no power running through it: Felix had listened closely and could hear no hum.

It was easier to walk single file. Felix was in front of Carolyn and listening idly to their footfall.

"Everyone's dead," she said.

"I know."

"Including my father."

"I'm very sorry. I know how you feel."

"That's the problem. I don't feel anything. It was just like this when my mother died. I was eight at the time and couldn't stop crying. That was when I underwent ERR. Maybe he was right."

"Who was right?"

"The president, when he had his ERR reversed. He was right to die in a natural state. Although I don't understand his remark about God. His last words were … delirious."

"Maybe that's the point."

She might have added more, but the tunnel broadened and they passed into an open space. It was brightly lit and in good condition. The wall's blue tiles were intact, as was its red brick floor and aluminum ceiling. Even its lettering was legible: King Station.

"Union Station's next," Felix said, pausing to survey the two subway platforms. The place was grimier than it had been two centuries before, but it was easy to imagine the commuters back then waiting impatiently for their train to approach.

"It's well preserved," Carolyn commented, reading his thoughts.

"Yes. It's what the world will look like a thousand years from now: all dressed up with nowhere to go."

"Let's keep moving."

"Good idea."

They continued walking. By now their feet were virtually sodden. At the same time their soles were aching because the tracks were uneven and pressed into their flesh. Still, they kept at it. Felix was imagining the men who'd constructed this tunnel, the work it had taken to blast through the rock and the expert engineering that had gone into the project. The president was right: when all was said and done humans were amazing. Not just the population that had travelled this subway, but the countless generations before them, the aboriginals who had crossed the Bering Strait, the Europeans who had come centuries later, the Greeks, the Romans, the

Jews, the Egyptians.... They had all known savagery and superstition, yet all of them without exception had contributed something to the human ... drama.

A far-off drone interrupted his thoughts. Glancing back, he could see flashing lights behind them, at a distance of maybe five hundred metres. The E.D.s had discovered the door to the stairwell, descended the steps, and were hot on their trail.

"Let's run for it," Felix murmured, picking up his pace.

Without answering, Carolyn followed suit. Spying a stretch of unbroken walkway, she leaped onto it and urged Felix to follow.

There was a sound of high-pitched beeping behind them: the E.D.'s' tracking devices had picked up their movements. They were four hundred metres away and closing in quickly.

"Halt!" a mechanical voice announced. "You are in violation of Presidential Order 3214T566 ..."

"There's Union Station!" Felix cried, as the tracks curved left and disclosed another well-lit space before them.

There was a blast a couple of metres behind and the tunnel in their vicinity exploded with light. An E.D. had shot at them with its long-distance stunner. The track's curve had removed them from its line of fire, but the drones would soon catch up.

There. Ahead of them stood the start of a staircase, like the one they had descended near the Queen Street station. Carolyn quickly mounted the steps, with Felix following a few steps behind. Again the structure wobbled beneath them.

"We're halfway there," cried Carolyn a minute later. Felix didn't answer. He was saving all his breath for the climb. He couldn't tell what was worse: his fiery lungs, his burning calves, or the feeling of dizziness as he spiralled upwards.

"Halt!" a voice echoed from below. The E.D.s were at the foot of the staircase. Felix heard a high-pitched whine, a sign they were ascending in pursuit of the pair. Thank goodness for the spiral: it would slow them down.

"I'm there!" Carolyn called, several metres above Felix. "And there's a box with a key! I'm working the door open...."

"Halt!" a voice thundered from nearby. "You are in violation of Presidential Order 3214T566 ..."

"Shut up!" Felix gasped. "You're just a machine!"

But this machine was moving in on him, with others close behind. It was three metres away, two and a half, two.... A whistle sang out as it charged its stunner and ...

"The door's open!" Carolyn yelled. "Watch it! It's right behind you!"

Felix could sense the E.D.'s presence — his hair was actually standing on end. He wasn't going to make it. He could sense its stun-rod was about to make contact....

He dropped onto his chest. Jabbing backwards with his leg, he struck the lead drone behind him. The machine was lighter than he had expected and was knocked back several metres. It collided with the second E.D. and created something of a domino effect as each drone crashed into the one behind it.

Taking advantage of this mess, Felix barrelled past the door. When the barrier closed, and the lock re-engaged, he practically sobbed with relief.

His feeling of reprieve lasted all of a second. Mounted to a nearby wall was a screen featuring the president's last speech. The sight reminded them — as if they needed reminding — that they were the very last humans to wander the planet. Despite their exhaustion, they stood and stumbled forward.

Their mission was far from over.

Chapter Thirteen

"Thermal reactor readings?"

"Normal."

"Plasmic interphase?"

"Normal."

"Temporal navigation signals?"

"All are above 1500 megahertz, except the one in delta sector."

As Carolyn paused to make an adjustment, Felix glanced up from one of three screens before him and gazed outside a viewing port. After reaching the depot, they'd discovered lines of shuttles lying in "dry dock." By moving cautiously, they'd managed to board one craft before the E.D.s had been able to "scope" them. Carolyn had a Class M license and, crippling the auto-drive, had piloted the craft to their destination. Within two hours of kicking the E.D. in the subway, they'd returned to the space station and the TPM.

"Are you alright?" Carolyn asked.

"Yes, of course," he answered, his gaze still directed outside. The infinitude of space stared back at him, its immensity so breathtaking, yet inhumanly cold. This void would not have seemed so chilling had he been able to speak to his mother; unfortunately she'd left a tearful message on their Holo-port, explaining that their supplies were depleted and the colony was as good as doomed. This awful message was three months old.

"Continue with the check list," he insisted, returning to the task in hand.

"Solar compression?"

"Normal."

"Radiation shields?"

"Engaged."

"Clavian vectors?"

"Optimal. Wait. Particle plane 2A7 should be altered point zero three degrees."

"Portal exits?"

"Energy deposits have been placed in two hundred and fifteen temples."

Not that they'd been able to relax. Their calculations had revealed the sun would reach a maximum output level within six-and-a-half hours of their arrival at the station; a delay would have required them to postpone another three days. Given the possibility of contracting the virus, they'd been forced to meet this very tight deadline.

That left them with the TPM. It was complex and beyond their operational skills. Luckily, upon entering its central chamber, they had spied a flashing Holoport that had screened a message from General Manes. Besides providing them with detailed instructions — in the unlikely event that they should return and attempt a second temporal projection — he had left a final message for his daughter. This was delivered after he'd held a scanner to his temple and, following the president's example, neutralized his ERR.

"My dearest Carolyn," he had said, speaking with an effort, "for reasons I never called into question, I have endured the reduction of my emotional range. As a result, while I've always watched your development with joy, I have never been able to say how much you meant to me. It has been expressed through countless gestures, of course, but the feelings were never set into words. Now, in my final moments, I want to state for the record that you, as well as your mother, have always been my sun and moon and stars and oxygen. If I have any regrets, besides the failure of our mission, it is that

I can't address these words to you in person. Continue fighting if you're still alive and pretend that I'm with you, cheering you on."

A few more words had followed, to the effect that he would blast his body into space, together with the other corpses on board, to reduce the chances of infection by the plague.

"Infra-red pattern analysis?"

"Normal."

"Geographical coordinates?"

"Longitude fourteen degrees, twenty-nine feet, ten point zero two inches, longitude forty degrees, forty-five feet, zero point zero two inches. Ancient Pompeii."

"Pompeii? Why not Panarium …?"

"Don't you remember what the doctor said? How there are no known temples in this second Panarium? Pompeii is the closest entry point."

"Okay. The coordinates are confirmed. Temporal insert date?"

"May 13, 71 BC, nine a.m. local time."

"May 13? That's three days later than our last visit. Why…?"

"The Romans will be fighting Spartacus's forces. Both sides will be too busy to interfere with our plans."

"All right. You know best. That means we're just about ready."

Rising from her console, Carolyn stretched. She was still wearing her jeans and sweatshirt, unlike Felix who'd changed into a new Roman outfit that he'd fabricated using the professor's program. Announcing she would be back shortly, she retreated to a changing room.

He stood and glanced outside again. He was thinking about their return from the past and their stop-off in that prehistoric era. It interested him that they'd been able to pause halfway to their destination. Perhaps this trick could be accomplished again. With a frown, he approached the chair that Carolyn had vacated and determined an additional set of coordinates. He just had time to punch these into the TPM's flight log when she stepped back into the room.

"Are you ready?" he asked casually, admiring the effect of her *palla* and handing her a pouch with cinnamon.

"No. But that shouldn't stop us."

They shook hands solemnly. To his surprise, Carolyn drew him close and squeezed him tightly. Wordlessly, she broke her embrace and they stepped into the TPM module. They triggered the ignition sequence via voice commands. The hidden circuitry started to hum, the plasmic interphase began to burble, the light was shifting to infrared and …

They were part of the twenty-third century no longer.

Chapter Fourteen

Felix blinked in the silvery shadows. He was recovering from the time projection and trying to get a fix on his position. Again they were in a narrow room, whose door was partly open and admitting streams of lights. The walls were of marble, as was the floor, and three statues were facing him — Minerva, Juno, and Jupiter. The air in the *cella* was dry and musty, and motes of dust were swirling about in an immaculate sunbeam.

"We're back among the savages," Carolyn groaned. She was shaking her head and straightening her *palla*.

"The sooner we find the flower, the sooner we leave."

They tiptoed to the exit. Determining the coast was clear, they left the chamber, crossed the stylobate, and descended three steps of travertine marble. Felix trembled visibly: they were standing in Pompeii.

They were looking out over the ancient forum. There was a concentration of stalls to their left — parading meat, fruit, fish, and other wares. Farther down, an attractive square beckoned, bounded at its far end by a large assembly hall. In front of them were administrative buildings; on their right a basilica and a second ornate temple, this one belonging to the god Apollo. Half a mile off was the Tyrrhenian Sea, at the sight of which he had to smile.

"What's the joke?" Carolyn asked, as they cleared the temple's steps.

"It's very strange. I've been here often and know the ruins well, and here they are in perfect condition. I would never have guessed the city was so beautiful."

"It is beautiful," she admitted.

"And it's funny how some monuments haven't been constructed yet, Eumachia's house and Vespasian's temple. And the sea is closer: the last time I was here — two thousand years from now — the water was three miles away from the city. Time travel has some very strange effects."

He led Carolyn to the south end of the Forum. Even as he admired the columns and stone of the buildings, he was surprised to see so few people about. Apart from the odd merchant, or the occasional cat, the city's streets and buildings were empty, as if everyone were taking refuge from some threat.

"It's like the world we left," Carolyn said. "Where is everybody?"

"There are people here," he answered, catching sight of a family through an open window. "Although in a hundred and fifty years, this place will vanish."

"What do you mean?"

"Look behind you," he said. "That volcano is Vesuvius. It's scheduled to erupt in 79 AD and will bury Pompeii in a thick layer of ash."

"I'm glad I don't know history; at least, I'm glad I can't see people's future."

"Believe me, I wish I couldn't see it, either."

They had reached the Forum's boundary and turned onto the *Decumanus*, the city's main east-west road. Unlike Rome, where apartment blocks were common, the buildings here were two stories tall with balconies that were exploding with the season's flowers. The road was wide and paved with flagstones that had been set in concrete. They passed a lovely fountain, too, whose water was supplied by a distant aqueduct — a feat of engineering that ran for sixty miles. And immediately past the fountain, they saw the public baths, a triple-arched structure that had been built to accommodate a crowd of hundreds.

"Chick peas! Peanuts!" an old vendor shouted, spying the pair.

"*Salve, senex*," Felix greeted him. "Where are all your customers?"

"*Salve, domine*. You are a stranger to these parts."

"You can hear it from my accent?"

"And your question. You haven't heard of Spartacus? How he commands an army as numerous as the grains of sand and treats all of Italy as his personal estate?"

"And that's why people are locked in their houses?"

"Yes. But he will learn his lesson when General Crassus arrives — as early as tomorrow, I've heard. But why are you here? You would be safer up north."

"We're looking for a man named Balbus. He lives in Panarium and —"

"Balbus? Of Panarium? *Domine*, I've never met the man, but a peanut shell would hold his luck with room left over for the nut within. Surely there is no one whom the gods hate more. Why do you wish to visit him — even Spartacus and his slaves have left the scoundrel alone."

"We are curious to see a man of such misfortune."

"In that case, carry food with you, unless you're prepared to eat the flowers in his fields. Indeed, you'd be wise to purchase my comestibles."

Felix nodded and ordered two large servings of chick peas. As the man spooned his wares into "cups" of plaited fig leaves, he directed them to Panarium. They had to leave Pompeii by the Stabiae gate and walk due south along the Via Popilia. At the 143rd milestone, a walk of eight hours, they would veer east on a *via rustica* for seven *milia passuum*. This secondary road would lead into Panarium, due south of which were Balbus's fields.

This said, the man handed them their chick peas. Felix gave him a generous pinch of cinnamon in return. The man's jaw dropped and he sputtered his thanks. He also offered them some parting advice.

"Be careful where you step. Spartacus is everywhere. There are some soldiers in the area, but their numbers are small and they can't offer you protection. In other words, you could be walking to your death."

Thanking the man for his concern, the pair walked off along the *Cardo Maximus*, a central north-south avenue that ended in the Via Popilia.

After passing two theatres and a gladiator barracks — all three structures had been abandoned — they reached the city's walls and emerged into a field. They found the start of the Via Popilia, which was four metres wide and beautifully paved. Felix felt a thrill when his feet grazed its surface: it connected him to every road across the empire, a network that was eighty thousand kilometres in length.

The pair walked aggressively for the next three hours, full of energy because they were heading toward their final goal. As fields and forests and craggy hills passed, they spied all sorts of animals that the noise from their footfall chased into the open: rabbits, mice, lizards, foxes, deer, and a snake with a zigzag dorsal pattern. Both were deeply impressed: the only place wildlife could be seen in their era was in the narrow bands of wilderness that were packed with tourists. Here, on the contrary, there wasn't a soul to be seen.

"There are no portals in Panarium," Carolyn spoke, in an effort to dispel the emptiness around her. "And I guess that means we'll have to return this way."

"It's not our only route. Once we've found the *lupus ridens*, we can walk to Paestum, which lies farther south. There are several portals there that we can use."

"I get the idea you're not so anxious to return."

"Are you crazy? Our world will die without the *lupus ridens*!"

"And if our mission weren't so urgent? Would you remain in the past?"

"Do you think I'm in any way attracted to the violence, slavery, and utter disregard for human life?"

"Yes."

Felix stopped walking. They were in a desperate hurry, but her statement went to the heart of his routines and raised a question that he had never quite answered. Why would anyone study the past? What good was served by examining the relics of half-baked populations that had sacrificed animals, enslaved their fellow man, fought neverending wars and believed the earth was flat? What was the attraction of such monstrous people?

"They are us," he finally spoke.

"What?"

"I much prefer our modern ways," he explained. "But I want to understand their evolution. The Romans are part of the human family, and I study them the way I would examine my parents...."

"They're not *my* family," Carolyn snorted. "I have nothing in common with them."

"If there were no risk of a butterfly effect, do you think you'd end up hurting people or maybe killing them in self-defence?"

"In a world like this? Sure. You would have no choice."

"So if our world were unstable, you would be as violent as these people."

"I don't know...."

"And if you were rich but had no robot to wash dishes, wouldn't you hire a human to do them? And if times were harsh, and the age's morals were different, isn't it possible you would own a slave?"

"What's your point?"

"I'm only saying we're not that different from the Romans. Take away our ERR, our robots, and our

cloning industries and you'd be left with people like
Crassus or Pompey."

He pressed forward. With a shrug, Carolyn followed
in his steps.

They said nothing for the next half hour, as both
were mulling his comments over, Felix no less than Carolyn. He was wondering if he'd said something profound
or ... imbecilic. His eyes roamed the countryside, which
was hilly and uncultivated and threatened to overwhelm
the road. A milestone passed — number 137 — when
finally the stillness was broken: a band of legionnaires
was mounting a hill.

There was nothing calm about their appearance:
they were wearing chain mail, helmets with prominent
cheek-guards, a *cingulum*, or belt, from which strips
of seasoned leather dangled, and *caligae*, or thick hob-
nailed boots. Each was armed with a rectangular shield, a
sword, and a menacing six-foot spear. There were twelve
of them and they were marching in step, as if they were
governed by a single mind. At the sight of their arms,
Felix's wound began to tingle.

"Should we run?" Carolyn asked, remembering the
soldiers who had tried to grab their cinnamon.

"I don't think so," Felix answered, with some hesitation. He was thinking that if they fled from this patrol,
they would have to abandon the road for the wilds and

might end up getting lost. Besides, even from a distance he could tell these soldiers were nervous, because Spartacus could assail them at any moment. This meant that they would not waste time harassing two young citizens.

The soldiers advanced, without checking their step. They were sweating profusely from their rapid pace of walking, and the road's dust was clinging to their exposed flesh. They were bristling with blades and metallic surfaces, their limbs were bulging with tanned, hardened muscles, and their eyes burned with a near demonic energy. Felix wondered if they should have run but it was too late to escape.

"*Ave, milites,*" he cried. "You have the road to yourselves."

One older, rough-hewn man with a badge on his belt gestured with his hand and brought the others to a stop. He considered Felix and Carolyn closely. After a moment's thought, he approached the pair.

"Why are you outside?" he asked. "Spartacus and his men are on the loose."

"We have urgent business with someone in Panarium."

"This is not the time for business, *puer*. Your lives are at stake." Felix met the soldier's gaze directly: he understood that the man, despite his tough appearance, was puzzled by their presence there and concerned about their welfare. At the same time, his companions were glancing skittishly about them, fearful of an attack that might arise at any moment. Clearly, they were anxious to keep marching forward.

"I appreciate your kindness," Felix said. "But duty calls us to Panarium."

"But you travel alone, with no servants, no food, no horses, no escort?" the soldier mused incredulously. "No, I can't let you — it would be equal to murder. You will come with us to Pompeii. When the slaves are beaten, you will attend to your business."

"But...!"

"*Adulescens*, my decision is final." To cut off any further debate, he whistled to his troops who drew the "guests" into their centre and started marching forward. Boxed in by these human shields, they had to move at the same pace as them, and a rapid step it was, desperate as these troops were to leave the region. While they were frustrated to be treated so, the pair did appreciate the soldiers' concern, especially when each was handed an apple.

"Have you been stationed in this region long?" Felix asked.

"We were in Spain five years," the leader panted. "And before that I served in Macedonia, under Sulla."

"The dictator?"

"Of course. I was with him when he marched on Rome, and before that he commanded me in the Social Wars — a dreadfully wasteful campaign. Why did Italians have to kill each other? I believe in our empire, but sometimes it comes at a frightful cost. Like this war against the slaves."

"You aren't ... enthusiastic?"

"Why should I be? If I were them, I would fight to win my freedom. Still, the Senate has dispatched us so who am I ...?"

He didn't finish his sentence. The group was rounding a bend in the road, which stood at the foot of a bush-covered hill. With a minimum of noise an army sprung from the earth above them, dressed in a mix of skirts and hides and armour, the latter captured in previous campaigns. Each was armed with spears and stones with which they viciously pelted the soldiers.

"We're under attack!" the veteran shouted. "*Adulescens*, this is no place for you! Take the girl and run into the wilds!"

He ordered his men to open their ranks and allow Felix and Carolyn to pass behind them. As soon as they'd retreated from their centre, the soldiers locked their shields together and prepared to meet their attackers head-on — a hopeless effort as they were grossly outnumbered. Without wasting a moment, Felix and Carolyn left the road and stumbled down a slope of scrub and undergrowth. As they crawled past bushes that were thick with thorns, they heard a series of cries behind them: the men on the hillside were on top of the Romans. There was an awful clanging as swords and shields clashed, together with curses and agonized screams. Never had Felix heard anything so dreadful.

As they slid toward the bottom of a gully, he looked back and caught a glimpse of the fighting. There were only five or six Romans left and they were battling dozens of Spartacus's men. One soldier fell, a spear buried in his neck. Was it the kind veteran? He didn't want to know; besides, they now had problems of their own.

"The scum is in the bracken!" someone called in Greek. "There are two of them!"

"There! I see the white of his toga!"

"We've been spotted!" Felix cried, slipping his toga from his shoulders.

"Down this way," Carolyn urged him, crashing into a cluster of shrubs. As Felix barrelled after her, he discovered, too late, that they had wandered off a five-metre drop; at its bottom was a channel clogged with mud and rotting logs. The fall knocked the wind from him. For her part, Carolyn struck the side of her head. Not only was she covered in dirt, but the side of her skull was bleeding profusely. Felix struggled towards her, a Herculean task as the mud was deep and thick as jam.

"It looks worse than it is," Carolyn mumbled, staring at the blood that was staining her tunic. He caught her as she lost her balance. Remembering her trick when he'd been stabbed back in Rome, he shaped a makeshift sling from her *palla* and, drawing the folds across his shoulder, hauled her to the high ground.

There were voices above him, around and in front. They didn't concern him; his priority was to escape the mud and staunch the blood from Carolyn's wound. He strained until he thought his shoulder would snap. Carolyn was dazed and could barely help him. A bird retreated from a nearby thicket, startling them both. He scrabbled upwards to a ledge of stone and, with the last of his strength, hauled Carolyn beside him.

"Did we lose them?" she asked, her face distorted with gore.

Instead of answering he gestured to their right. Three grizzled men with half-bared chests were wielding spears whose tips were pointed at their throats.

Chapter Fifteen

Felix could barely feel his legs. He'd been walking for at least six hours over very rough terrain. Every time his step had slackened, he'd been pushed from behind by one of his captors or slapped or kicked or viciously insulted — it was generally believed that he and Carolyn were spies. He'd been given a crust of bread to eat and only once been allowed to drink from a stream. Compared to Carolyn, he was lucky. Her skull was bandaged with a strip from her *palla* — the rust-coloured stain on the cloth was horrific — and she was so groggy that her step was uncertain. To keep her going, he'd given her his piece of bread. He'd wanted to comfort her with words as well but a guard had threatened to stab him if he spoke.

They were travelling with a band of men who, to elude all Roman troops in the region, had been avoiding the main road and cutting across the countryside. When this had proven difficult — some hills were impassable — they had travelled on the Via Popilia and headed in the direction of Paestum. They'd even passed milestone 143 and the rustic road that led to Panarium. Felix had eyed it yearningly. A lug of a slave was watching him, however, and escape at that point was out of the question.

But where were they headed? Focusing his thoughts, Felix visualized a map of ancient Italy. They were moving toward Paestum, and had passed the town of Picenti. That meant Salernum was coming up, Eburnum next, the river Silarus ...

The Silarus. Of course! How stupid of him! That was where the slaves and Romans would fight and Spartacus would make his famous last stand! So they had to be getting close to his camp. He was going to say as much to Carolyn, but the lug caught sight of him and whacked him hard.

"You mangy, cursed Roman! One word to the girl and it will be your last!"

"I've told you already!" Felix snarled. "We're not Romans!"

"Of course you aren't! You only dress like them, and

smell like them, and travel with their soldiers. But you aren't Romans, no, heaven forbid!"

"My sister speaks no Latin! I'll prove it to you ..."

"I said don't speak to her!" the lug barked out, lifting his arm to hit him again. Before he could strike, a scout called out from a nearby hill. He was standing with a couple of guards who had appeared from out of nowhere and was motioning excitedly.

"We're here, lads. Home sweet home!"

The group moved forward and climbed the hill. For all his tiredness, Felix gasped when he reached the crest. Below him was a long, wide meadow that had a stream meandering through its middle. This space was packed with makeshift shelters, built from blankets suspended on networks of branches. Herds of livestock were standing about, with dogs watching over them to prevent them from straying. And ten thousand bonfires were burning at once and beating back the onset of dusk with their glowing embers and plumes of smoke. While these details and many others gladdened the eye, they were nothing compared to the masses of people who were sprawled across the landscape like a swarm of locusts.

On and on their numbers ran, for as far as the eye could stretch, tens of thousands of human souls. The bulk of them were men who were armed to the teeth, but there were plenty of women and children too. Felix was surprised to see so many non-combatants present, his assumption being they would impede the defenders, but in actual fact they had services to offer. Former slaves, they were skilled and used to hard labour and could provide high quality "logistical support." They were tending the livestock and feeding the army, cleaning the equipment and looking after the wounded. They were imposing order where there should have been chaos.

"This is incredible," Felix said. "You've built a city out of nothing."

"Hear the spy!" the lug declared. "He counts our numbers and assesses our food and observes how cunningly our camp is arranged."

"I keep telling you. I'm not a Roman. Listen to my accent!"

Instead of answering, the lug shoved him forward and they entered the camp. As they walked past endless tents and fires, they drew lots of attention. Some slaves gazed with sympathy at Carolyn, who looked miserable in her tunic and blood-soaked dressing. When the lug announced she was a Roman, however, their kind looks turned to ones of hatred.

Wending their way past shelters and fires and chicken coops and forges and horses and children, they came upon a Roman tent: it was made of leather panels tied together with guy ropes.

"Magonus!" the lug called out. "Have a look at the Roman scum we captured!"

The lug was large and bursting with muscles, yet seemed puny alongside the brute who emerged. He was six foot eight, weighed three hundred pounds, was bare-chested, dressed in trousers and wore his white-blond hair in two plaited braids — the traditional fashion of Gauls, Felix knew.

"Your hunting was successful, Borgo?"

"We dispatched a patrol then grabbed these agents, even though they tried to escape us."

"Put them in with the other Romans."

"But we're not Romans ..." Felix started.

"The stockade is too good for them. We should kill them now!" To emphasize his point, he gave Felix a smack.

"You savage!" Carolyn growled.

"What was that?" Borgo bellowed, rounding on her. He didn't understand Common Speak, but recognized when he was being insulted. He swung his arm to whack her too. An instant later he was on his back, blinking in confusion and gasping for breath.

"Translate for me," she told Felix. "If anyone harms us, I will hurt this man."

"What's she saying?" Magonus asked. "And what language is she speaking?"

"It's called 'Common Speak,'" Felix said. "And we

use it in Prytan. My sister is warning Borgo to keep his hands to himself."

"You two are from Prytan?" Magonus asked. "I thought you were Romans. After all, you were seen wearing a toga."

While hiking, Felix had concocted a tale that would explain their actions and dampen the slaves' resentment. He started with the usual "facts" — how their father was a Druid and how he'd been sent to live with Romans to study their ways. At this point he began to embroider: after he'd been absent a year, his sister had joined him and their troubles had started. Their host had fallen in love with her and wanted to divorce his wife and marry her. When Felix had refused — she'd been betrothed to someone else back home — the Roman had locked them up in his house and sworn he would keep them there until they met his demands. Happily, they had managed to escape. To avoid detection, Felix had "borrowed" a toga and pretended to be a *civis Romanus.*

"But why are you here?" Magonus demanded. "You should have headed west for Prytan, and not travelled to Campania."

"We are Druids," Felix answered, having expected this question. "We have a legend that speaks of great things to come when a wolf-like flower sprouts instead of grain."

"Enough talk," Borgo growled. "Spare us your lies."

"The point is," Felix pressed on, "we have learned that such a flower grows here in Campania and wish to see if it is the one our legend speaks of."

"So you have risked your lives for a flower?" Magonus asked. His voice was full of doubt and laughter.

"Yes."

"Don't listen to them," Borgo cried. "They're spies for the Romans and —"

Magonus held up a hand and Borgo fell silent. This mountain of a man stepped over to Felix and lifted him effortlessly so that their noses were touching. Training his fierce blue eyes on his, he stared straight into him, as if to search his very essence out. After a minute of such scrutiny, he set him down.

"There is truth," the giant murmured. "But there is something else."

"Then it is as I said!" Borgo yelled in triumph. "Kill him and the girl!"

"No," Magonus mused. "We will test him. Follow me."

The giant strode off from his tent, passing through a crowd of slaves who had gathered to see what this drama portended. Carolyn released Borgo and followed after Felix. Even with the bandage on her head, her muddied clothing, and a feverish stare, she projected a quality that stirred respect in the onlookers.

They walked along the meadow, passing women

who were cooking, men who were inspecting weapons, a throng of children who were teasing a lamb, and youths who were playing a variety of games like *tesserae*, *terni lapilli*, and others. Although a hundred details vied for his attention, the one that struck Felix most was the variety of languages being spoken around him. Latin was the most common one, but mixed in with it were snatches of Greek, Hebrew, and ancient Persian, as well as tongues that were utterly remote, Dacian maybe, Noric, Phrygian, Illyrian, Aramaic, Punic, Celtiberian. He understood how his father had felt when, wandering various parts of the world, he had stumbled on collections of books that neither time nor neglect had wiped from the planet.

His father. If only he were there, he was thinking. If only he could hear these words and the two of them had time to piece their meaning together.

Magonus's hand broke in on his reverie. By now they had reached the far end of the compound and were standing before a large stockade. Behind this barrier was a crowd of Roman soldiers — numbering in the hundreds at least — who'd been stripped of their armour and were clad in simple tunics. They were weak, dirty, and grossly unshaven. Some, like Carolyn, were covered in blood, while others were dying or dead already. Surrounding this palisade was a crowd of jeering slaves — young kids for the most part — who were yelling that they didn't

look so tough without their weapons, that they hadn't
expected slaves to defeat them, and that these same slaves
would one day raze Rome to the ground.

Ignoring the crowd, Magonus walked up to this
"jail" and motioned one of its inmates over. He was a
muscular man with dark, curly hair and a hawk-like face
that had once been handsome, but was gaunt with hunger now. Fearfully, the man approached the Gaul, who
signalled to some henchmen. They dragged the Roman
to a space outside the prison and pinned his arms behind
his back. Magonus nodded to Borgo who unsheathed
his sword and threw it to the ground in front of Felix.

"Take that sword and kill the Roman," Magonus said.

"I beg your pardon?"

"Kill him," he repeated, looking Felix in the eye.
"Your willingness to do so will reveal your intentions.
Quickly. Night is falling and there is work to be done."

Felix looked at the sword, then at the curly-haired
Roman: the man was clearly terrified but was intent on
dying honourably, without moans or tears or pleas for
mercy. Felix could imagine the thoughts passing through
his head: how he wished he could bid his family goodbye,
how he was sorry before the gods for any crime he'd
committed, and how he wasn't yet ready to surrender
his ghost....

"Take the sword!" Magonus thundered.

"What's the matter, spy?" Borgo jeered. "Perhaps you know this Roman scum?"

Felix glanced at Carolyn, then at the crowd around him. Clearly, he couldn't kill this man. Besides the risks of a butterfly effect, the idea of driving steel into a stranger and watching his blood spurt and hearing the air leave his lungs, no, all of this was out of the question. He looked at Magonus.

"I can't violate the sanctity of human life."

"What?" Magonus thundered, as the crowd unleashed a flurry of cat-calls.

"My tribal ways have taught me that to extinguish a life is to extinguish a world. What you ask is impossible and irreligious."

"Very well," Magonus laughed. "Borgo was right. You are a spy...."

"Let me kill him," the lug offered.

"That would be too easy," Magonus chuckled. "Instead, let us arm this soldier. If he wishes to live, he will kill the spy. If the spy desires life, he will forget his principles and destroy his opponent."

The surrounding crowd roared with approval. Gathering torches, they settled in to watch a *munus*, only this time Romans would be fighting each other. As Borgo found a sword for the Roman, a slave armed Felix with Borgo's weapon. Carolyn wanted to intervene, but four men seized her and she was warned — through Felix — that involvement on her part would lead to instant execution.

Again, Felix's wound was tingling.

"Let the game begin!" Magonus cried, dropping a scrap of fabric to the earth.

The Roman charged Felix. He was weak with hunger, but his desperation lent him strength. He stabbed with his sword, not once, but several times in quick succession. Instinctively Felix protected himself, blocking each blow with his own length of bronze, and flinching as sparks travelled the length of their blades. Despite his lack of training, he was quick on his feet and able to dodge the strokes — his experience playing halo-ball was useful. If the soldier had been fed and rested he would have made short work of him, but in his weakened state he kept missing his target. He was also tiring quickly. The spectators laughed and insulted the pair, words to the effect that the Roman empire would crumble with effeminate soldiers like these to defend it.

Stung by these insults, the soldier drew himself straight and brought his sword down full force on Felix. Twisting like a fish, he dodged the attack and watched as his opponent tumbled to the soil. That was when he dropped his sword and faced Magonus with a look of contempt.

"Of all people, you should know the loathsome nature of such combat. And yet you copy your enemy's worst sins, and rob your cause of all its justice. Despite your freedom, you're still slaves to your passion!"

"You know nothing of slavery!" Magonus thundered. "How dare you tell us what is right and wrong! Kill him, *miles*," he urged the panting soldier. "And we will let you live and see your wife and children!"

Unable to believe his luck, the soldier mustered his remaining strength. His sword upraised and gleaming murderously in the torch-light, he fell upon Felix. He was neither grateful for his show of mercy, nor in any way reluctant to stab his benefactor. From far away, a million miles away, Felix heard Carolyn calling his name, even as he prepared for the steel's final kiss, the agony as his soul was ripped from its moorings, and his final gasps as the shadows claimed him....

It wasn't to be. There was a rush of motion and the Roman fell backwards, knocked off his feet by a well-aimed stone. Felix cringed, sure that Carolyn had interfered, and that death would be visited on both of them now. But no, she was still in the grip of Borgo's henchmen. Who ...?

A tall, lean figure jumped into focus. There were no surviving portraits of the man, no sculptures, no mosaics, no paintings, no frescoes, but Felix knew his identity well, as surely as if he'd been looking at his very own father.

And so he caught his first glimpse of the gladiator Spartacus.

Chapter Sixteen

Felix woke to the sound of muffled voices. It was black around him and the air was rank with sweat and garlic. He was perspiring beneath a woollen blanket, his legs were sore, and his right temple was throbbing. Sitting upright, he strained to catch his bearings.

"We've lost half our men since the winter snows melted."

"But we're thirty thousand strong still."

"For two years we have plundered, with what end in sight?"

"To teach the Roman scum a lesson."

"Surely our purpose is nobler than that. And won't they learn a lesson if we retreat from Italy and return to our homes?"

It was all coming back to him: the long march, the camp, his match with the Roman, and Spartacus's dramatic arrival on the scene: with a look of disgust, he had ended the *munus* and insisted that their "guests" be properly received. When Magonus had declared he wouldn't share his food with Romans, and the other slaves had murmured their agreement, Spartacus had decided to host the pair. He had led them to his tent in perfect kindness, where they'd been fed and washed and their wounds had been treated.

"We can't leave Italy until Rome is in ruins."

"Do you suppose, Magonus, we will win such success? Rome is strong and will never be beaten."

"Our cause is just."

"And our homes are sweet. Let us disband while fortune smiles on us still."

"I disagree. We must fight. Are you with me, boys?"

As a chorus of men expressed their approval, Felix considered the bundle beside him. Carolyn. She'd had a hard night. Feverish and restless, she had tossed and turned and talked in her sleep — several times she had called out to her mother. He remembered groping in the dark for some water and giving her a drink and wiping her forehead. Eventually she had slept like a stone.

Reassured to see her fever had broken, Felix crawled toward the tent door and pushed the leather flap aside.

Stepping into a perfect summer's day, he shielded his
eyes from the low sun in the east. The tent had been
pitched on the verge of the meadow and confronted
him with the pretty sight of ferns and scrub and knee-
high grass, whose blades were bright with the morning dew. Behind him were innumerable encampments,
whose inhabitants were beginning to stir. To his right
was a bonfire, around which several men were huddled.
Among them sat Spartacus. Although he wasn't the
biggest man in their circle, a subtle glow enhanced his
features and marked him as their natural leader. As if
sensing Felix's gaze upon him, he raised his eyes and
took his presence in.

"Our guest is up," he announced. "Let's include him
in our council."

"So he can tell our plans to the Romans?" Magonus
sniffed.

"Make room, Boaz," Spartacus addressed a thin,
bearded figure. "He will sit next to you."

With a smile of embarrassment, Felix sat with the
captains.

"Let's continue," Spartacus said. "Please excuse us,
Felix, if we mention facts that are not known to you."

Felix smiled at this apology. Little did this leader
guess that he had read Appian, Plutarch, and other writ-
ers, who had chronicled Spartacus's slave rebellion. In

other words, he was intimately acquainted with the man's history. His grin quickly faded, however, as the gravity of their situation struck home.

The slaves were at the end of their tether. They had recently arrived in the Silarus valley after losing their captains Castus and Crixus together with a huge number of men. Spartacus had won a battle soon after, but at the cost of an additional ten thousand troops, leaving him with thirty thousand warriors in all. For his part, Crassus had six full legions, and reinforcements would be arriving soon. The conclusion seemed obvious: they were fated to lose. This was why Spartacus wanted to flee, dissolve the army, and make his way home.

"Crassus is a brute," he was telling his generals. "And that Roman brat Pompey has never been beaten."

"We bruised them before," Boaz spoke. "We can bruise them again."

"And we can use the river as a defence," Gannicus added.

Felix started when he heard the river mentioned. Far from serving as a bulwark, it would be a tomb for these slaves. His expression grew more downcast.

"Felix," Spartacus said, desperate to find someone who would agree with his plans, "you seem to me the thoughtful sort. What do you propose? Should we meet the Romans in combat, or should we run to the north?"

"He's a stripling and a spy," Magonus rasped. "His voice shouldn't be heard at our council."

"Magonus is right," Felix stammered, wishing he could speak the truth and save the army from annihilation. "I am ignorant of war. Consider your friends Crixus and Castus, both seasoned warriors who were worsted in battle. How can I advise you when such leaders failed?"

"The boy's no fool," Magonus laughed. "Although I'm not acquainted with these men he speaks of."

"Perhaps he refers to Mors and Dolor," Boaz said.

"Perhaps," Spartacus mused, with a neutral look. He was about to add something, but was interrupted. A gangly teen broke in on the group, dressed in a tunic and a shirt of rusting mail. His hair was matted and grass was clinging to his clothes. His news was urgent, but he was self-controlled. Felix knew the Romans had been spotted.

"Forgive my intrusion," he gasped, "but Crassus draws near."

"Already?" Magonus barked. "I thought we had time to prepare."

"We count six legions," the scout continued. "At their present rate of progress, they'll be here in three hours."

"Let's have a look," Spartacus sighed, climbing to his feet. Calmly and methodically, he told his captains to arrange their units for battle. As soon as they were fed and mustered, they would march due north along

three different routes, concealing themselves in the surrounding hills. When they had advanced two miles, they
would await his instructions.

As his captains scurried off, he asked if Felix could
ride a horse. When Felix answered no, he said his horse
would bear them both and that they would ride to take
a look at the Romans. He then directed him to awaken
his sister and to eat a quick breakfast so that they could
leave soon. These orders given, he called for his horse.

Returning to the tent, Felix saw Carolyn just outside its entrance. She was bleary-eyed and bruised all
over, but her expression signalled she was fit for action.
Relieved to see that she was feeling better, he led her
toward a fire pit where three bulls were being roasted on
spits. As they walked, he explained how Crassus's troops
were advancing and Spartacus wanted them to scout
things out. Carolyn nodded vaguely. She was distracted
by the tumult and couldn't focus on this news.

By now the camp knew the enemy was close. With a
discipline and energy that would have impressed Crassus,
everyone was setting about his appointed task. Some
were packing up the bedding and tents, in case they had
to leave in a hurry. Others were carrying helmets and
breastplates, which they fitted on the fighting population,
wishing them luck, kissing them repeatedly, and voicing
fervent prayers aloud. Swords, spears, and shields soon

followed, and men who only moments before had been talking to their wives or dancing children on their knees were transformed into engines of destruction.

And it wasn't just the men who were intending to fight. Boys younger than Felix were holding bows and slingshots. Their features were a curious mix of fear, resolve, and … optimism.

A girl handed Carolyn a handful of daisies. "To celebrate our victory," she explained with a giggle.

"Will they win?" Carolyn asked, once the girl had scampered off.

"They will be ground into the dust," he replied grimly.

There was nothing further to say, so the two approached the fire pit in silence. Each asked for a serving of meat and watched as a man who was stripped to his waist carved thick slabs from a bull's dripping haunch. Wrapping these in leaves, he handed them their breakfast. He smiled when they thanked him, and said he hoped the meat would give them the strength of a bull.

"I'm not hungry," Carolyn said, staring at the food. "These people seem nice and I don't want them to die."

"I don't either," he agreed. "But we have to eat."

As if to underline this point, Spartacus came over, with Boaz close behind. He was dressed in scaled armour and was heavily armed. He was also mounted on an ivory white charger that was eighteen hands tall, had a huge barrelled chest and was bulging all over with veins and muscle. His name was Thrax and he was beautiful.

"Climb behind me," Spartacus called, extending his hand to Felix. "Your sister will ride with Boaz. Quickly. We haven't much time."

With no choice in the matter, Felix grasped his hand and leaped toward him. In a practised motion, the warrior swung him up, causing him to land towards the horse's rump. There was no saddle, no stirrups, only a coarse woollen blanket. With no other means to keep himself steady, he wrapped his arms round Spartacus's waist. Smiling at his helplessness, the general advised him to cling to the horse with his thighs. After Carolyn was seated on Boaz's mount — she too was grasping him round his waist — Spartacus produced a clucking noise. Instantly Thrax set off at a trot.

Like most people of his era, Felix knew little about animals. He had come upon dogs and cats only rarely, and knew horses only from pictures in books. As Thrax raced off, he couldn't believe its power, its surefootedness on the rough terrain, not to mention its astounding endurance. When the beast hit a canter, he clutched Spartacus so hard that the iron on his breastplate left marks on his skin.

"Be sure you don't strangle me," he called out.

They rode the full length of the camp, passing crowds of slaves who were getting ready for the day's campaign.

Long columns of men were leaving the meadow and streaming into the neighbouring hills, many of them fitted with Roman equipment, but many dressed in gladiatorial gear, sturdy leather skirts, or reinforced tunics. All were stepping lively, and all looked fierce and full of bluster.

Thrax left them behind. Mounting one hill, then another and another, its hooves clattering against the sun-baked earth, the horse muscled forward as if toward a formal finish line. It was so used to Spartacus's clucks and gestures that Felix thought they were one beast combined, a centaur whose human half could detach itself at will. There wasn't a soul about, apart from Carolyn and Boaz some twenty yards behind.

They rode for half an hour. Advancing on a hill that was the steepest in the region, Spartacus reined Thrax in and dismounted with the grace of a dancer. Boaz and Carolyn appeared moments later, and Spartacus ordered them to stay with the horses. Bidding Felix to follow him closely, he started up the scrub-covered slope, his scabbard jiggling against his calf. The hill was steep and set with loose stones, but Spartacus was fit and climbed without pause. For his part, Felix thought his muscles would seize up: his attempt to cling to Thrax with his thighs had turned his hamstrings to the hardness of marble. Wincing at each step, he did his best to keep up.

After climbing a few minutes, they reached the summit. Once there, Spartacus lay upon his stomach, sheltering behind a wall of scrub. Felix joined him and surveyed the valley below. It paraded fields of wheat and barley with a road down their middle — it was like a zipper on an old pair of pants. Because it was summer the wheat was two feet high and swaying hypnotically at each gust of wind. There were very few trees and even fewer houses, and all livestock had long been driven off. Hugging the horizon was the river Silarus, a band of brilliant silver in the early morning light.

In the distance six squares were stealing over the plain, each a mile long and evenly spaced from its neighbours. Clouds of dust dogged each mass like a shadow, and pinpricks of light struck Felix's eyes, from the sun glinting off a thousand points of metal. While these squares weren't moving at a rapid pace, their momentum seemed unstoppable, and the innumerable spears and swords and arrows proclaimed their target would be cut to pieces. They watched the Romans' progress in silence: if Spartacus was intimidated by this show of strength, he was doing a fine job of concealing his fear.

"They're about to dig in," he said, as the columns stopped their marching and wagons pulled into view. "I wonder how many camps they'll form. Three, I think."

"Five," Felix spoke.

The legions deployed themselves across the plain, attended by their engineers who plotted out the camps' dimensions. They were bent on building five fortifications.

"Isn't it interesting," Spartacus mused. "That you guessed the number of forts correctly."

"Pure luck," Felix replied, cursing himself for speaking out of turn.

"It's funny, too," Spartacus went on, "how you spoke of the captains Crixus and Castus. You referred to them by their given names, and not by Mors and Dolor, the nicknames they were known by. Very few people know this information."

Felix's mouth was suddenly dry. Spartacus's gaze was burning a hole in his skull.

"And there's a slave from Prytan who heard you speak to your sister. He said your language is not spoken on his island."

"I'm not a Roman," Felix croaked, swallowing hard.

"That much is obvious."

"And I'm not your enemy."

"Instead of saying what you aren't, tell me what you are."

Felix weighed his options, as he watched the Romans. He couldn't tell this man the truth, and yet he couldn't lie outright to him. With a sigh, he tried to find a point in the middle.

"I've been burdened with a dreadful task, one more difficult than the battle that awaits you." Felix looked the general in the eye. "Billions are depending on the success of my mission. If I fail, if I don't reach Panarium, the entire human race will die, in Italy, in Prytan and everywhere else. Although my story sounds preposterous, the health of my world hangs upon a simple flower."

For a moment they exchanged stares with each other. Spartacus's features were impossible to read, and Felix was thinking the man had every right to stab him, or to burst out laughing at the tale he'd been told. At the very least he would have him arrested, either as a spy or, worse, a lunatic. Unexpectedly Spartacus looked away and considered the legions in the distance.

"You know how this will end," he observed, as if stating a fact. "I can see it in your eyes. You can divine the future."

"I can divine the past," Felix replied.

"Will we win? Will we prevail today?"

Felix spoke with caution. "There will come a time when no man will be able to enslave his brother. Years from now, remembering leaders like you, people will appreciate the worth of our souls and will guarantee each man his personal freedom. This will come to pass, as surely as the sun will rise tomorrow."

"I understand," he said slowly. "You are saying we will lose but that, in some way, we will win."

He climbed to his feet, with a near drunken look. Reaching into a pouch that dangled from his belt, he rummaged inside it until he produced a golden ring. Kissing this, he handed it to Felix, who saw that it was embossed with the figure of a horseman.

"This is for you," he announced. "In heartfelt thanks for the news you've delivered. It is not every day we learn our fate, and the messenger of such bearings must receive his due — even if he speaks of death."

"I spoke of life, too," Felix protested.

"So you did," he said, with a mournful smile. "But let us leave this place. It would appear I am fated to lead my army to defeat."

Chapter Seventeen

It had been an hour since Felix and Spartacus's exchange and in that interval the slave had been a whirlwind of activity. His priority had been to ride to his troops and order them to move into a forward position: two divisions were to muster on the Romans' sides and attack as soon as the signal was given, three flaming arrows in quick succession. He himself was leading the third division and had marched them to the hill that he and Felix had climbed. At its base, he'd arranged them into twenty cohorts, each containing six hundred troops, and deployed these in an unbroken line: it was a mile long and ten ranks deep. Magonus held the right flank, Gannicus the left, while Spartacus assumed command of the centre. Because it was noon already, his captains advised that they wait until the next day to attack.

Spartacus disagreed. He argued that any lengthy delay would allow the Romans to complete their camps and that they should go on the immediate attack.

"Although we can still change our minds," he suggested, "we can march to the north, dissolve our army and allow every man to make his way home."

"If we disband," Magonus answered, "the Romans will find new people to enslave."

"This is a war to the death," Gannicus agreed. "Either we die or the Romans do."

"In that case, we'll fight," Spartacus said with a shrug. "I just hope the gods are well-disposed to us this day."

He motioned to a contingent of boys who were dressed all in white. Because the slaves had no cavalry, these boys had been directed to precede the army and fire on any horsemen that approached. Having organized the troops, he motioned Felix over.

"Climb this hill and observe the battle from its crest," he advised. "Wait until the sun is halfway to the horizon, then proceed due east as fast as you can. After you've covered five miles, turn north and continue to Panarium. Avoid travelling on the diagonal as it will be thick with Romans. And take this."

He handed him his toga, which had been laundered and repaired. Its folds were damp but would dry out in the sun.

"If you meet any Romans, they'll assume you're one of them."

"You have our thanks," Felix croaked, his voice heavy with emotion.

Spartacus nodded. He was about to move away when, just as suddenly, he pulled Felix to him.

"Remember me," he whispered, practically crushing his ribs. "I will survive somehow if you keep me in your memory."

"I'll remember you," he gasped. "I give you my word. Your presence will be with me till my dying breath."

"Then farewell, Felix. May the gods smile brightly on your task, and may you only know the glow of freedom all your days."

Without another word, he turned away. As he stepped toward his beloved Thrax, a young boy handed him a metal helmet, a bowl-like contrivance with a blood-red crest. Fitting this on, he led his horse forward.

His troops were muttering and looked downcast. Now that they were on the verge of battle, they were skittish and uncertain of themselves. One thickset man blocked Spartacus's path and confronted him, his arms akimbo.

"The rumour is you'd rather run than fight," he cried, in a tone loud enough for dozens to hear. "Is that why your horse is trailing behind you? So that you can flee if the Romans defeat us?"

Spartacus paused and considered the man. A thousand pairs of eyes were witnessing this scene and he could smell the numbing fear taking root in his troops: clearly a gesture of some kind was necessary. He sighed and drew his sword, causing his challenger to retreat a step. Instead of attacking the man, he turned and kissed his horse. As Thrax nuzzled him back, he drove his sword into his breast, killing him instantly as the bronze met his heart.

"I am now without a mount," he cried, as Thrax shuddered involuntarily and fell to the soil. "I hope you will accept this as a pledge I won't desert you."

Felix and Carolyn jumped in shock, horrified by the sight of blood and the beast's last spasms. The troops were startled but murmured with approval, while the thickset man fell to his knees and begged the general's pardon for having doubted his courage. Squeezing the man in reassurance, Spartacus raised him to his feet and climbed a nearby boulder.

"I have often heard it said," he declared, in a voice that travelled the length of his army, "that the Romans have been graced with wisdom, hence their mastery of the world's populations. And yet for a people so wise, they must be fools, because this day they fight a battle that they are fated to lose. Yes, my dearest friends, these legions that thirst to tear our hearts from us cannot possibly achieve victory this day. Consider their purpose:

they wish to steal our liberty and make us slaves again. It seems a simple task, yet is as hopeless as returning spilled wine to its bottle. If today we rout our foe from these meadows, even they will admit that they have failed in their quest and we are not dumb beasts to be deprived of our freedom. And if fortune proves fickle and their swords should prevail, not only will death release us from their shackles, but they shall know by our willingness to die in battle that we value freedom above life itself. Both in victory and defeat they shall find themselves worsted.

"My friends and fellow freedmen, our time beneath the sun is short. From cradle to grave, we seek our purpose. What is man? What reason do our struggles serve? The tears we have shed, the toils we have shared, what monument do they raise, what gods do they ennoble? I don't know. I cannot say. There is one sole truth I grasp, and one alone: I have your trust, I have my freedom, and I will fight for both until the sword is pried from my hand. War awaits us. Let us march. Death is not unwelcome if I die by your side."

The effects of his words were marvellous to behold. From downcast and stooped, the troops were standing straight and cheering themselves hoarse. Without further ado, Spartacus hastened to their front and led them forward at a rapid trot. Felix and Carolyn climbed the adjoining hill and found a perch on its crest where they could watch the proceedings — not that Felix had any doubts how this struggle would end.

"This is crazy," Carolyn said. "They can't find a better way to settle their disputes?"

"They will not be slaves."

"I'm talking about the Romans."

"They have problems of their own."

"It's so brutal, all of this. Are you going to watch? I don't want to witness the death of these people, never mind which side they fight on."

"It would be … dishonourable not to," Felix said, although the idea of watching Spartacus fall pained him deeply. "My father always said that history is an act of friendship. I never understood what he meant … until now."

They fell silent. By now the slaves were well into the meadow and were formed into their three divisions, each marching alongside the other and with a twenty-metre gap between each group. Each was further divided in three: the front line's purpose was to absorb the foe's onrush; the second was expected to go on the attack; while the third, consisting of the truly hardened troops, was to hold the soldiers in tight formation. These were tactics that mirrored the Romans' own.

The Romans. As soon as scouts had seen the slaves advancing, there'd been a blast of trumpets and the troops had left off work on their camps, grabbed their weapons, and arranged a battle line. Their discipline was breathtaking: three minutes after they had spied the slaves, they were charging forward in an orderly fashion: six rectangles, each with six thousand souls, were converging on the slaves from different angles.

"I see Spartacus," Carolyn said, using her retinal enhancements. "And Crassus is urging the Romans on."

"He can't believe his luck," Felix groaned. "He didn't think Spartacus would meet him in battle."

The Roman cavalry charged ahead of the legions, and were met by a wave of archers and slingers. A number of knights were knocked from their horses, or were forced to retreat when struck by a hail of arrows, but others reached the archers and inflicted havoc: points of white lay still on the landscape, like boundary stones marking the start of Death's dark realm.

A hundred metres yawned between the armies, then eighty, fifty, twenty, ten. Like hives of rabid bees converging, the masses finally clashed with a din so loud that the crash of bronze on bronze was like a world-shaking thunderclap. Although the forces were too far off for him to spy in any detail, Felix could tell their roiling, boiling masses were wreaking terrible violence and shedding blood by the buckets. The sun was reflecting off a million points of metal and the cries of men fighting and killing and dying rolled into a wall of sound that seemed solid enough to bruise an onlooker's skin.

Several times each line threatened to buckle, only to regroup and redouble its fervour. As Crassus sent two legions to charge the slaves obliquely, three flaming arrows ignited the heavens and, from their positions in the surrounding hills, Spartacus's reserves poured in from the sides, like the jaws of a wolf snapping closed on its prey. Viewed from afar, this mass of half-crazed humans was like a monster drawing its first breaths of air, its infant lungs heaving backwards and forwards.

"The sun is halfway to the horizon," Carolyn cried. "We should think of leaving."

"Let's wait a few minutes. Where's Spartacus?"

She squinted and saw him ranging in the front lines. Wherever his men were weakening, he urged them to hold fast, even as he lashed out fiercely at the Romans. He was tireless and pushing as hard as he could.

"Magonus has been wounded," she reported. "There's a spear in his shoulder. Wait, he's lifted a Roman and is swinging him in circles. He's knocked five soldiers down … he's plucked the spear out and … three more Romans have been battered. His men are taking courage … oh, he's been hit in the throat … he's on his knees … the Romans are swarming him … his men are resisting, no, they're moving back."

Felix closed his eyes. He was sweating profusely, yet trembling with cold. Although he'd known from the start the slaves would lose, it was nightmarish to see them fall in battle, just as it was horrible to watch so many Romans die. If they knew that, down the road, every human on the planet would be threatened with extinction, would they shelve their differences and stand together?

Carolyn was nudging him. He opened his eyes.

"Spartacus is charging Crassus!" she cried. "He's gathered some men and is rushing the general! I can see his crest bobbing up and down. He's thirty yards from Crassus and is cutting through the troops."

"I can't see." Felix was squinting until his eyeballs hurt. "It's all one quaking, bloody mass."

"He's rushing forward … he's twenty yards and getting closer. Crassus sees him … his troops are fighting back … he's smashing them … wait, he's hit … no, he's charging still … he's ten yards off. The Romans are massing … his men are dropping off like flies … he's lost his helmet and …"

"That's enough," Felix said, jumping to his feet. "It's time to leave." That said, he bounded down the hill and starting running east.

He knew what was happening. Ten yards off from Crassus, Spartacus was face-to-face with hordes of Romans, without a single friend to back him. Two centurions were hounding him like wild dogs. Killing one, he was struck by the other, just below the ribs. As he stabbed out, he kept calling to his men, but they were too far off to rally. Crassus was yelling, "Kill him! Kill him!" A hundred blades were lunging at Spartacus, striking his legs and arms and chest. The light was fading. His lungs were tasting his last breath of air, and his heart was pumping faintly, faintly … it had stopped. And now the Romans were trampling him like a doormat as they muscled forward to liquidate their adversaries.

The world was filled with death, Felix was thinking. Spartacus was gone, his men were being slaughtered, and, two millennia later, the plague would ravage everyone. He thought about his father, lying on the lawn. His mother had died on Ganymede's cold surface for want of food and oxygen. General Manes was gone, the professor was gone, the doctor, too, and everyone on earth….

"Felix! Wait! Don't race ahead!"

He couldn't help himself. He was running like a panicked deer. The world was closing in on him, war was closing in on him, time and fate and death were closing on him, and, if he dared stand still for even a second, they would wrestle him down and grind him to powder.

He ran and ran and ran. He threaded through some hills and, when these ended, he dodged a tract of woodlands for the space of two miles. A stream blocked his way — a branch of the Silarus — but he splashed across its waters and charged through mud, scrub, sand, and sharp stones.

"Turn left," Carolyn panted, as they reached the boundaries of a modest town. "Panarium is north."

Veering north, with the sun sinking in the west, he ran full tilt, his chest on fire. On and on he stumbled, passing houses, barns, and rustic shrines. Some farmers were carrying a bundle in a winding sheet, their heads bent earthwards in a show of grief. A funeral. Yet more death. It was squeezing out his oxygen, but he couldn't stop running, not to drink, not to rest, not to pay his respects.

"Felix! The sun's setting. It's getting hard to see."

He entered a field with grazing cows. The animals scattered before his advance, their lowing either protests or advice to take it easy. But they didn't know, they couldn't guess, that death was in pursuit of them, too, otherwise they wouldn't chew grass at their leisure. He jumped an ancient boundary wall and charged across a field of grain, certain that death was hiding in among these stalks. He crossed a second stream and barrelled through an orchard, his feet hammering the senseless earth, his eyes trained squarely on the far horizon, to a point in space that he could never reach, not before death had claimed him for its own.

Then Carolyn tackled him. The sun was gone, the moon hadn't risen, and he would break a bone if he continued. They fell to the earth and a bed of green received them. He struggled to stand, but she pinned him to the soil, both of them panting and soaked with sweat. For minutes they lay there, her hands refusing to let go, yet conveying, for all their roughness, a tenderness her ERR would normally suppress.

And then they slept, their arms wrapped tightly round each other.

Chapter Eighteen

The sun was rising and had a blood-red tinge. Felix stirred beneath its rays and discovered that Carolyn was curled against him. He was faintly embarrassed but grateful for her warmth: the earth was freezing and the morning dew had soaked his toga. At the same time he appreciated the ... closeness of her presence.

He glanced around him. Where ...? They were lying in some farmer's field. Unlike the neighbouring plots, it contained no grain or vegetables, but was filled instead with a simple flower....

His heart practically stopped. Squirming free of Carolyn, he picked a flower and studied it closely. Yes, no doubt about it, the petals resembled a smiling wolf in profile. He gave a resounding, heartfelt whoop.

"Carolyn! Wake up!" he cried. "We've finally made it!"

"What is it?" she groaned. "And don't start running again...."

"We're in Balbus's field! We've found the *lupus ridens*!"

Carolyn climbed to her feet and surveyed the terrain. Spying the flowers' telltale pattern, she managed something close to a smile. Not satisfied with this show of emotion, Felix grabbed her by the waist and danced with her, spinning her in circles as a million "laughing wolves" looked on.

"What now?" she panted, coming to a stop.

"We'll find a temple," he gasped. "In Pompeii, no, in Paestum. It's fifteen miles away and probably our best bet."

"Fifteen miles? We can get there by this afternoon. I just wish we had some food on hand, because the last time we ate was yesterday morning."

"I'm starving too. In fact ..."

He raised a flower and bits its petals off. As Carolyn watched him in disgust, he chewed energetically and swallowed the mass down.

"Come on," he urged her, reaching for a second one. "We know it isn't poison. Besides, if we're infected with the plague, we should eat these flowers to stop the symptoms from erupting."

With a disgruntled look, she bit into a flower. While its petals had a faint sweet taste, the stalk was tough and difficult to swallow. Still, their hunger was so pressing that they ate until they had sated themselves. Gathering multiple samples of the plant, they wrapped them into the folds of their clothing and secured the bulges with double knots. This task done, they quit the field.

Their legs were stiff from the previous day, and, because it was cold and their clothes were damp, the first few miles were difficult. Gradually their muscles slackened and the sun warmed them up. The sky was a hospitable blue and the landscape was attractive. Most important, they were close to completing their mission.

"Maybe this world isn't so bad," Carolyn spoke.

"Oh?"

"I'm not backtracking now. I still think these ancients are hopelessly backward, and their superstitious practices are ridiculous. But I'll admit there is something admirable about them. And, I suppose, I envy them their freedom."

"I don't follow."

"I mean their freedom to express their emotion. I live in a box with this ERR. I know it keeps me and others from exploding, but I wouldn't mind experiencing true emotion for once...."

She broke off as a woman came running toward them, cradling a newborn. She looked distraught and on the brink of collapse. Spying the pair, she came to a halt, not knowing whether to turn about or to flee straight past them.

"It's okay," Felix called. "We're not going to hurt you."

The woman didn't move, as if hoping they would take her for a corpse or statue. Her baby bawled a little, but it was weak with hunger and its wails were thin.

"We were with Spartacus," he declared. "I promise you, you're safe."

The woman studied him. She was twenty years old but had the carriage of a crone, as if her youthfulness had buckled beneath her tribulations. Her hair was matted, her skin was filthy, her clothes were rags, and her sandals were ruined.

"They've lost," she cried. "For all their strength, they've been cut to pieces."

"I know. I'm very sorry."

"The Via Appia is lined with the survivors. The Romans have crucified six thousand men and have left them to die a slow, painful death...."

Felix was silent. There was nothing to say.

"There are Romans everywhere," she wailed. "They will track me down, if I don't die of hunger. They will enslave me, and my child will never know freedom. But I must go! I can feel their breath upon my shoulders!"

With a shriek she barrelled past the pair and vanished

into a nearby orchard, her step as unsteady as her future prospects. Unable to help her, they pressed forward.

Their mood only darkened when they stumbled on a corpse minutes later. A man was sprawled inside a bush where he had taken shelter. He was steeped in blood, the result of a wound to his neck. And that was just the first of many bodies. Farther on, they found a string of victims, all of them still and soaked with crimson, although their faces seemed to register contentment, as if each were happy to be leaving this world.

"How many of them are there?"

"Hundreds," Felix answered. "And their numbers will grow as we get closer to Paestum."

"What about the Romans?"

"They're here, too. Let's hope they don't bother us if we happen to be spotted."

But they were seen soon after by a wandering patrol. And far from ignoring them, the legionnaires closed in on them with barks of triumph that were far from friendly.

"Should we run?" Carolyn asked.

"I don't think so," Felix mused. "They'll pursue us and ... look," he said, pointing in the distance where a second band was lurking. Escape was out of the question.

"What have we here?" the lead soldier shouted, as he and his men surrounded the pair. They were sweating freely and covered in dust.

"Thank goodness you've arrived!" Felix yelled. "We thought you'd never come and they would find us again."

"Who?" the soldier asked.

"The slaves, of course."

"Well, there's no fear of that," he smirked. "But how do we know you're not part of that gang? Your accent's foreign."

Felix laughed. "We have friends in Paestum who'll vouch for us — and they'll pay a reward when they see we're alive."

"A reward?" the soldier crowed. "Why didn't you say so? We're on our way to Paestum ourselves and would be happy to escort you. Wouldn't we boys?"

His companions agreed, opened their ranks and drew the pair into their middle, to prevent them from escaping their clutches. As they moved off at a rapid clip, Felix told his usual tale — how they were from Prytan and were of Druidic descent. The lead soldier explained that they were part of Pompey's legions and had arrived too late to fight the previous day, a pity because they hadn't received any spoils.

"But your friends in Paestum will look after us," he said with a laugh.

They passed more corpses littering the landscape. As the troops discussed the successful campaign, and marvelled that Spartacus had at last been defeated, Carolyn asked Felix what he was planning. With a smile, he told her not to worry. These soldiers would escort them safely to Paestum, where he would ask their permission to enter a temple and extend proper thanks to the gods, a request they wouldn't dare refuse. Once inside, they would return to the future and deliver up the *lupus ridens*. Carolyn nodded and expressed her approval.

After walking for a couple of hours, they stumbled on Paestum; one moment they were climbing a hill, the next they were advancing on the town's central gate. Towering over the *vicus* were three handsome temples — dedicated to Neptune, Hera, and Ceres. Felix was too distracted to give them more than a glance: deployed outside the walls were crowds of Roman troops. At their centre was a figure in a blood-red cloak.

"Is that who I think it is?" Felix asked.

"It is," Carolyn answered, using her retinal enhancements.

"Maybe he won't see us. Just keep walking and don't look his way."

"Here we are, Paestum," the lead soldier cried, conducting them to the start of a gate whose arch was about to swallow them whole — and so deliver them from Pompey's notice. "Where do your friends live?"

"They're near the temple compound. In fact ..."

Felix was nervous and not watching his step. He

tripped against a flagstone and knocked into Carolyn, who in turn struck a soldier whose spear tripped his neighbour and caused him to fall with an ear-splitting clatter. Laughing heartily, the soldiers helped their mate to his feet. They were just about to continue forward, when a thunderous voice brought them to a halt.

"Well, well," Pompey cried, approaching on his charger. "So the gods do indeed bring villains to justice. That's why they tripped you and brought you to my notice."

"*Imperator*," the lead soldier spoke, "we are conducting these citizens into Paestum for their safety...."

"At ease, centurion." Pompey laughed. "How could you have known these two 'Romans' are spies when they duped even me and my senator friends? But their lies have ensnared them. They will join Spartacus in hell and send him my fond greetings. Execute them instantly. That will teach them to challenge the authority of Rome, and to betray a host who showed them only kindness."

Pompey's words transformed the soldiers. A moment before they'd been the pair's protectors; suddenly they were rough-handling Felix and pinning his arms and drawing their swords. They were gripping Carolyn, too, who'd been caught off guard and was utterly helpless. The flashing sun against their swords was blinding Felix. Within seconds these men would slit his throat and with that gesture the human race would end.

Unless ...

"*Imperator*," he yelled, as Pompey was wheeling about on his horse. A blade was poised two inches from his throat. "How is your wife Julia?"

"What's this?" Pompey asked, stopping abruptly. "I have no wife Julia. You are mistaken, boy."

"I'm not speaking of the present," Felix gasped. "I'm referring to your future bride, the daughter of Gaius Julius Caesar."

"Are you mad?" Pompey cried, riding back to him and staying the lead soldier's hand. "What's this rubbish you're spouting?"

"I suppose it is rubbish," Felix continued. "As is the fact that you'll be chosen consul next year, together with Marcus Licinius Crassus. And then there's your fight against Mithridates...."

"This is insanity! Lucullus leads our armies against him...."

"But you will end the war in the east, just as you will personally defeat the pirates, when the *lex Gabinia* grants you *imperium*."

"I ... this is preposterous ... let them go!" he yelled at his men. They were only too glad to obey — they didn't like the idea of killing a Druid. As Felix caught his breath and straightened his clothes, Pompey eyed him with loathing and ... fear.

"Who are you that you dare tell my future? Speak quickly boy, before I have you crucified."

"I'm tired of this talk of death," Felix growled, in a voice that matched Pompey's bullying tone. "As I told you, we are Druids. The gods readily grant us a vision of the future."

"Boy, you try my patience!"

"Mind how you address a *vates*, *imperator*!"

"You! A prophet?" Pompey sneered. "Why should I believe you?"

"We can prove it." Felix shrugged. "Lead us to a temple and the gods will manifest their love for us. If they refuse, your soldiers may do as you command. But be warned, *imperator*: any man who harms a priest forfeits blessings from above."

He and Pompey exchanged stares with each other. Normally there wasn't a man alive who could endure the glance of Rome's leading general; Felix returned his gaze, however, and even caused Pompey to lower his eyes.

"We go to Neptune's precinct," he announced. "But if your claim proves false...."

This threat was left hanging as Pompey dismounted his horse. Without speaking further, he strode through the gate, motioning to his troops to follow. Immediately past the arch was an open space with twin temples standing side by side. Crossing an expanse of polished marble, the troops kept a gap between themselves and Felix, not wanting to jostle him if he was a true prophet.

The pair reached the temple steps and climbed to the top. When Pompey wished to follow suit, Felix warned him in a sombre tone that no mortal could follow where they were going. He also offered the general a piece of advice.

"Your future, as well as Rome's, is both difficult and glorious. But nothing lasts forever and the power that will end your empire will not be swords or spears or catapults or fire, but the Roman appetite for blood and wrongdoing. Where kindness is forgotten, decay soon sets in. And now for that proof that we are agents of heaven. *Vale, dux,* and may you know only blessings."

He crossed the stylobate, with Carolyn in tow. Walking past a single row of columns, they drew near the *cella* and opened its door. As Pompey's men cried the *cella* was off limits, they passed into the darkened space where a statue of the god Neptune beckoned. Before approaching this statue and entering the portal, Felix hurried to a distant corner, took out Spartacus's ring and crouched down on his hands and knees. Feeling out a crack between two pavement stones, he shoved the ring inside it and pushed it down several inches. He filled this crack with dirt and pebbles then hurried back to Carolyn's side. Without exchanging a word, they stepped forward together.

There was the slightest breath of wind as time received them in its embrace.

The usual tunnel of light opened up and again their limbs were impossibly distorted. Although his eyeballs were like two strings of putty, he could just make several details out. The first was a patch of shadow in the distance where the gleaming console from the TPM was visible. Carolyn was moving toward this goal and about to regain her place in the future. But even as this opening pulled him, a second "patch" revealed itself and disclosed a scene that was even more familiar.

It had worked, Felix thought in triumph to himself. When he'd punched a second set of numbers into the flight log, mere minutes before their second trip to the past, he hadn't been sure this time and setting would appear, but there it was in front of him. With an ease that came as a pleasant surprise, he was able to steer his limbs to the "patch" and gaze into the scene it disclosed.

It was even better than he'd hoped.

He was staring into the garden at home. Nothing had changed since he had seen it last, the vegetation, the statues, the projection of tranquility. And over there — Felix experienced a thrill — his father was dozing beneath an apple tree and a crow was calling to him. On the staircase at the far side of the garden, he could see himself standing and watching his father, his face twisted with fury at the crow's mocking laughter. It was all as he remembered it to be, that afternoon before his father fell ill. How strange the universe was, that time could be looped on itself like a length of common string!

But he had to hurry if he was going to set things right. Concentrating hard, he fumbled with his toga and worked a flower from inside its woollen folds. He then thrust his arm forward into this realm, even as he called to his father.

"Dad! You have to listen! Dad! Can you hear me?"

"Yes," his father answered in a dream-like tone. "What is it?"

"I know this sounds strange but it's very important. When you awaken, you'll find a flower at your feet...."

"What's that raucous sound?"

"It's a crow, that's all. When you see the flower, you must hide it in your pocket."

"Hide the flower," his father murmured.

"That's right. But don't touch it until you end up in a Medevac. At that stage you must eat it, stalk and all. Do you understand?"

"Is this a joke?"

"No. Please. I know it's crazy, but do as I say. And you can't discuss this when you go inside. I mean, you can't say a word to me. Not a word. Do you understand?"

"Yes."

"Do you promise?"

"I promise."

"Otherwise … we'll lose you."

"You have my word."

Felix was going to add something further, but the tunnel he was in was starting to shimmer and he didn't want to press his luck. Retracting his arm, he steered himself down the glowing tunnel and headed toward the TPM. Carolyn could be seen and her limbs were normal, an indication that she was safe. But what the …? The patch was contracting. Like a match whose flame is sputtering out, the door to the future was growing dimmer and dimmer.

He focused hard and pushed himself. Would he make it? He wouldn't make it. The patch was shrinking faster and flashing at its edges. It was four metres wide, three, two, one … it was fading, it was shadowy, it was the barest of outlines.

An arm appeared — it looked like a spaghetti noodle — and grabbed his toga and pulled with frantic strength. With a thousand eras shrieking all around him, he felt himself fly an inestimable distance until he crashed against some tiles like a sack of potatoes....

Four pairs of eyes stared down at him.

"I was wrong," General Manes spoke. "That toga doesn't suit you."

Chapter Nineteen

The shuttle was drifting over downtown Toronto; its buildings looked spectacular in the early morning light. Although they were tiny at that distance, pedestrians were visible in the city's streets and were strolling about in sizeable numbers. Lake Ontario was sparkling in the distance and everything looked fresh and filled with potential, as if the world had been created that very dawn.

Only yesterday President Gupta had announced, from the Assembly Hall in the World Federation Center, that the virus had been comprehensively defeated. After praising the globe's population for its courage in adversity, he had added, to tumultuous applause, that citizens could circulate and travel at will. Dispersion Portals had been opened and shuttle service had resumed.

These changes hadn't happened overnight. The delivery of the *lupus ridens* had been the first of many steps. Biologists had studied its genetic structure and gradually determined its chemical "ingredients." A sample vaccine had been mixed together and tested on a group of simulated patients. When these had proven one hundred percent successful, the cure had been tested on genuine humans, and, given the positive results, had triggered the synthesis of vaccine on a massive scale. Within three weeks of receiving a dose of *lupus ridens*, patients had experienced a reversal of their symptoms and been fit enough to leave the Wellness Centres. Although the world wasn't back to normal yet, the streets were full of people, vehicles were running, shops were open, and, all in all, civilization had been saved.

"You're in a good mood," Stephen Gowan observed, from a pod across the aisle from Felix. He was thinner, his eyes were sunken, and his skin was faintly pock-marked; his swagger was intact, however, as was his condescension.

"Who isn't feeling cheerful? We survived the virus."

"I knew we would find a cure," he said in a matter-of-fact tone. "It was touch and go for a while, but science saved us as it always does. What book is that?" His tone was openly rude and dismissive.

"I'm reading the *Aeneid* still. I almost have it memorized."

"Despite the crisis you're still continuing with your studies?"

"Of course. Why wouldn't I?"

"I would have thought the threat of death would make you want to be useful. I myself will take chemistry more seriously in future. But I suppose people like you are stuck in a rut."

Felix considered Stephen. He was tempted to tell this arrogant buffoon exactly what he'd accomplished with his language skills. His words would have been a waste of breath, however, and at the same time landed him in serious trouble. After expressing heartfelt thanks, General Manes had reminded him to keep the facts to himself, to the extent that he couldn't even tell his parents. "No one can know about the TPM," he'd insisted. "And I mean no one." Still, his silence was a small price to pay for the plague's disappearance.

His thoughts were interrupted when a call came through on his Teledata screen. It had been a week since his father's release, and three days since his mother's return from off-world, but he still couldn't believe his family was together. To see his parents on the screen like that, grinning and energetic and full of life, filled him with indescribable joy. He remembered the sight of his dad on the lawn, and his mother's message that her supplies had failed. How strange to think that their salvation, as well as the well-being of every human on the planet, had depended on an ungainly flower.

"You're off early!" his mother said. "You left before breakfast."

"I have something to do."

"Will you be in time for your lesson?" his father asked.

"Are you up to it? You're supposed to take it easy."

"I'll take it easy by reading the historian Tacitus with you."

"Leave time for me," his mother broke in. "I'm hoping we can spend a week by the sea. It will help us recover from the recent ordeal."

"How about Crete?" her husband suggested. "We could tour ancient Knossos?"

"Or the island of Cos," Felix added. "I'd love to see the Asklepeion."

His mother laughed. "I don't care where we go as long as I'm beside the sea and can enjoy a beautiful sunset. But let's leave it up to Mentor. I've programmed in our separate wants and I'm sure he'll come up with a great location."

Felix grinned. When he had arrived home, he had immediately seen to Mentor's repairs. As soon as the computer had come online, he had subjected Felix to a thorough health scan and puzzled over dirt that he'd detected in his hair and nails: after observing this residue was two thousand years old, the computer had down-loaded a series of programs to correct an obvious soft-ware glitch.

"Don't be long," his mother urged. "We have lots of catching up to do."

"As well as lots of reading," his father joked. "See you later."

His parents disconnected. Felix was about to muse again how strange the events in recent days had been, when yet another call came through. This time it was Carolyn.

"So we did it," she said, "The world is back to normal."

"It looks that way."

"And I suppose we live happily ever after? Everybody returns to their routines, and forgets the fact that we were on the brink of extinction?"

"Do you really think people will forget so quickly ...?"

"They will. You'll see. We belong to the future and always blank out the past. A week from now there will be no reference to the plague, not in the news, not from the president, and not in people's conversations. It will be as if the crisis never happened."

"But it did happen. That's all you have to tell your-self. The past is always there, underpinning the present, whether we absorb it or not."

"I guess that's a comforting thought." She paused, as if nervous to continue. "Look. I want to see you."

"I want to see you too."

"Can we meet this Sunday? We'll go to Pompeii and tour the ruins. And maybe ..."

"What?"

"Maybe you can teach me Latin."

"Really?"

"I keep thinking of the time we spent together. And, well, I keep thinking of you. I'll see you Sunday, maybe?"

"You bet. Bright and early. And ..."

But she'd broken off contact. Felix glanced at Stephen Gowan, who caught his gaze and snickered to himself. Almost feeling sorry for him, he looked out the window at the scene below. By now the shuttle was cruising over Labrador, whose landscape looked gorgeous in the morning light. If he'd been glad before, that was nothing compared to his happiness now in the wake of Carolyn's call.

He couldn't wait for Sunday to arrive.

He was perspiring heavily. Despite the forecast for rain that afternoon, the temperature was eighty five degrees, true to the Automated Weather Bureau's forecast. He could have avoided this heat by using the Dispersion

Portals, but had wanted to reach his destination on foot. That was why, after he'd landed in Rome and taken two shuttles to the town of Laura, a centre known for its beef-cloning farms, he had proceeded to walk. From Laura he had travelled three miles on Route 21 (formerly Poseidonia Street), and two more miles on Route 46 (the old Neptune Road), which was taking him due east, exactly as planned.

He was getting close, he thought, passing a hand across his brow. Despite the alterations the terrain had undergone, to accommodate the pipes that ran for hundreds of miles, each bearing nutrients for the cloning process, he felt the landscape looked vaguely familiar. This suspicion only mounted when he reached Route 63 (Magna Graecia Lane) where, directly north, he saw two ancient temples. Despite his fatigue, he broke into a run.

There. Standing by the side of the road, where the remnants of a wall were visible, he grasped exactly where he was. Twenty-three hundred years before (or four weeks ago if the TPM were factored in), Pompey's soldiers had almost killed him on this spot. Walking past the wall — and disturbing a small lizard — he approached the open precinct where Neptune's temple greeted him, its columns still miraculously standing, even though they'd eroded since he'd seen them last. He climbed the stairs to the stylobate, expecting to see Pompey hovering nearby. It was from this place that he'd addressed the general, warning him Rome's prowess would inevitably fail. And indeed it had, in the intervening month.

He walked toward the temple's interior. Much as he'd expected, the *cella* had collapsed and its blocks of stone had long been carted off. By studying the floor, he could easily make its outline out. It was the traces of its back wall that interested him most. He crouched and inspected these cracks in the floor.

There was a lot of dirt, much of it hard-packed, and it concealed the joins between the marble paving stones. For the next few minutes he brushed it with his fingers. He also took a knife from his pocket and poked its blade into a multitude of cracks.

Nothing. It was too much to hope that in the intervening centuries, given the thieves and archeologists who'd visited this region, his "deposit" had survived.

The sweat was pouring freely from his scalp. He shook his head and half climbed to his feet, frustrated and ready to admit defeat. But it was then he noticed a thin line of mortar that was almost, but not quite, the same colour as the stone. He frowned. It had been poured between the original blocks three hundred years earlier to fortify the temple. He used his knife to scrape at this mortar. It crumbled easily, weakened by repeated heat and rain. Pushing his blade as far it would go, he ran it slowly the length of that join and almost choked when he heard a faint metallic "ping."

He excavated a hole wide enough for one finger. He stuck his index in, groped about and finally extracted … a metal ring. Its surface was covered with greenish mould but, here and there, a spot of gold shone through. Feeling hot and cold at once, he rubbed its signet and peered at the pattern that emerged: it showed a warrior mounted on a horse. Tears stealing from his eyes, he raised his face toward the sun.

"I remember," he whispered. "I'll never forget."